Debora Schafer was born in Devon, England and in 1990 came to Australia back packing with a girlfriend. Having a break before heading home they stopped off at a small town called Tully on the East coast of Queensland heading to Mission Beach. That's where she met her husband to be, as he and a friend stopped and offered them both lifts on their motorbikes.

Debora married her Australian man and has lived in Australia ever since, raising a family.

To Dougie and Liam, without you I would never have experienced this beautiful country.

Debora Schafer

THE LOVE OF A GRIFFIN

AUSTIN MACAULEY
PUBLISHERS LTD.

A CIP catalogue record for this title is available from the British Library.

ISBN 9781786129789 (Paperback)
ISBN 9781786129796 (Hardback)
ISBN 9781786129802 (E-Book)
www.austinmacauley.com

First Published (2016)
Austin Macauley Publishers Ltd.
25 Canada Square
Canary Wharf
London
E14 5LQ

Dedicated to Judy Tate (book lover) for proof reading
the manuscript and telling me to carry on.

Chapter 1

Katrina's ears popped, as the wheels of the plane hit the tarmac with a large thump.

"At last, Townsville!" Abbey said, grinning beside her.

"That's the first step of our journey over, now for the long drive. Let's hope the air con works, Kat."

Abbey Hammond had always called Katrina Kat, from a very young child and because she could never pronounce Katrina. The nickname stuck and then her brothers picked it up too.

"I wish we could fly the rest of the way, we would be there by lunch. Saturday will be over by the time we get there and I hate using my time off travelling," Abbey said. Kat laughed at her best friend.

"Unless you have a helicopter's licence that I don't know about and then a helicopter, then no, we won't be flying!"

They taxied along the runway and pulled into the number six stop, avoiding running over the guy with the flags trying to park them by the terminal building. After the air stewards opened the doors they left the plane and went to retrieve their luggage.

Once all their belongings had been put on the trolley, the two girls made their way to the car hire booth. Abbey had booked a four-wheel drive Toyota Land Cruiser as they needed to go off the bitumen and onto dirt road later to get to Abbey's place.

Katrina had not been back to her home town, to visit her parents in over twelve months. As a nanny caring for two small children; Alex, 8 months and Martha, nearly four. She did not get a lot of free time, she really had chosen a very demanding career. Their mother had died when Alex had been born, leaving the rock star singer dad to cope on his own. Rob would tour for weeks at a time, so unless Katrina took the children with her, during her time off, her days off were limited to when he was home. And two days would not cover the travel time it would take her to get home and back.

Katrina applied for the job knowing all this so she could not grumble. It did have its perks; Rob loved his kids and sometimes insisted they joined him on small tours. Never in her life would she have dreamed part of her job would include travelling on a private jet. The last tour took them to Tokyo, Hong Kong and back to Sydney and finishing where they started, in Brisbane.

"Kat! Earth to Katrina Cross." A pair of dark blue eyes were looking at her with concern.

"Sorry, just thinking about the kids, I hope he can handle it."

"Come on, we only have two weeks to relax and enjoy, it will be gone before we know it."

They loaded the Land Cruiser with their luggage and jumped in. Once out of the airport and through the city, they pulled in to a MacDonald's rest stop to get supplies; they needed drinking water, food and a good coffee. It was going to take them about one and a half hours to get to Charters Towers and then another two and half hours to get to Twin Hills. Abbey got her mobile out and called her parents to let them know they were on their way and to see if they needed anything. Katrina had already checked in with hers once she got off the plane.

They were both adults at twenty-two, and had both grown up out in the bush, but their parents were always worried about them when it came to travelling; Vehicles could break down, and there were no rest stops for hundreds of kilometres. When you wanted to see another driver for help, there was never anyone around and you could be hours waiting on the side of road. There was also very little phone coverage, so that meant if you didn't know anything about cars you would be stranded.

The first part of the journey flew past, and before they knew it Abbey was driving through the outskirts of Charters Towers. Abbey pulled into the fuel stop on the high way and Katrina got out to top the tank up.

"Next stop Twin Hills," Kat yelled over the car. Abbey looked at her and said.

"Yeah, and I bet your Dad's got a list of jobs ready for you?" She laughed.

Dad had always wanted Kat to get involved with the hospitality industry but she had other plans. She wanted to see the world, and did not wish to stay in one place for too long. She certainly was not going to stay in a small town for the rest of her life, where everyone knew everyone's business.

Twin Hills was a small town with a population of around a hundred and fifty people in the middle of nowhere, under the protection of a mountain range. It had once been a large fossicking area, back in the gold rush. The tourists still came out every year to go panning for gold in the creeks. There were a lot more nuggets to be found, if you knew how to use a metal detector. Twin Hills was approximately two hours' drive out west from Charters Towers. It had a hotel, a bar, a post office, a bank and a supermarket. Any larger items needed for the cattle properties were either brought in on road trains from Charters Towers or Townsville the larger city.

They drove into town just as the sun was going down, the street lights where coming on to show them a little more clearly that the tiny main street of Twin Hills with its row of shops all lined up like soldiers was still the same, after all these years. Nothing ever changed here, or so Katrina thought. Kat wound down the window to look around and noticed the temperature was dropping for the night. Winter was on its way.

Abbey pulled up in the hotel car park and they got out.

"Wow, it's freezing out here, let's get inside."

Katrina's dad, Charlie, saw them from the bar and came running out to meet them in the hallway.

"Girls, it's been so long!" He picked his daughter up in a bear hug and swung her around before putting her down.

"Hey Dad, it's so good to be here, it's been too long."

"Hey, Charlie, how's it going?" Abbey said as she was hugged and swung around too.

"Mary's getting ready to open the restaurant. Go in and say hello! I will unload your bags."

The girls found Mary in the dining room, they both squealed and ran and hugged her. Mary just held them both in a large embrace with tears in her eyes.

"Hello girls, it's been too long, it's so good to see you here at last. We are full tonight, new people in town just bought Harris's property. Are you going to stay tonight, Abbey? You can bunk in with Katrina."

"No I will keep going. Jared and Andy will be waiting for me!"

Katrina walked her out and watched her climb into the car. As Abbey took off down the road, her hand out of the window waving to Kat, she had a feeling she was being watched, with goose bumps rising up her arms she ran back inside.

The hotel bar was full as she entered, and after throwing the luggage down in her bedroom and grabbing a jumper, she went in search of a cold beer. It had been a long day which had started at 4.30am. Katrina walked in behind the long wooden bar and poured herself an xxxx lager. Dad was busy talking to Patrick, one of the locals, about last night's footy game, but winked at her. She walked over to give him another hug and say, "Hello!" to Patrick, and could feel the hairs on the back of her neck stand up.

Her body felt hot and her heart was racing. She felt danger for her father but did not know why. She looked around the room to find a young guy with dark wavy hair and strange-looking golden eyes, staring, or rather, glaring at her. She thought it was silly as she had never seen this guy before, but her stomach was tied up in knots.

He was sitting over in the corner with two companions and after he said something to them, they all turned around to look at her. They all seemed to have the same dark wavy hair down to their shoulders. Two of them had bright blue eyes and the other, these glowing golden ones. She thought she could hear one of them growling, but no one else in the room seemed to notice so she dropped her eyes, embarrassed, finished her beer and took off to find her mother.

Mary was in the kitchen with the cook, overseeing the evening meals for the customers. After a small hug, she got back to work. Kat asked if there was anything she could do and was told by her mother to go and freshen up with a hot shower, after the long day of travelling, which she was happy to do.

"We will eat after the rush, honey," she called out as Katrina headed for the door.

"Okay," she said looking over her shoulder at her mother and walked out into the hall. Not watching where her feet went, she tripped over the breakfast trolley and fell straight into a hard chest.

Her body automatically went to straighten back up but was held in a circle of large strong arms. Her eyes looked up from the muscular body into the eyes of her captor and gasped, it was the young guy from the bar. His eyes were not glowing any more, but replaced with the most beautiful eyes she had ever seen, they could only be described as hazel, with lots of bright golden flecks.

They seemed to hold her, demanding Kat's full attention, all she could do was look straight into them, and she was putty in this stranger's embrace. His body trembled as he grabbed her and received a small hit of electricity through his arms; it ran straight into his nervous system.

A saucepan lid dropped, rattling to the floor in the kitchen, making her jump and bringing her back to the present. She shook her head and was slowly released from the iron grip. He bent down, touching her ear with his sweet breath and whispered, "Mine," then disappeared down the hall back towards the bar.

The hot shower was so good, it relaxed her and calmed the nerves she had brought to the surface. When she closed her eyes all she could see was his eyes, staring back at her.

What just happened? Who the hell was that guy? And what did he mean, 'Mine'! she thought angrily. She was no-one's, and that was the way she liked it. How dare he! After she dried herself off, and found some fresh clothes in her case, she went back down stairs.

Trying to avoid another encounter with the seriously hot stranger, Kat went straight to the kitchen; even if it meant hiding there all night she was going to do it.

Hailey was still cooking guest orders so she started to wash up. By 9pm the dining room was empty and it was their turn to eat.

Being with her parents again reminded her how much she had missed them. Her father made sure all the customers were served with drinks in the bar before coming and joining them at the table.

"Well this is nice, Katrina honey, it's really good to see you," Charlie said, squeezing her spare hand.

"Thanks, Dad, it's good to be here, I'm sorry I can't get home more often but you know how it is."

"The new owners of Harris's place were asking about you!" Kat nearly choked on the wine she was drinking.

"What?" She looked shocked and could feel her face going red and ears pricking. He laughed at her.

"You have interested one of the Williams brothers, I am not sure which one's which. With names to faces, he might be the older one. Anyway, you can find out."

"One of them wanted to know who you were and who I was in relation to you, he also asked if you were staying long."

Katrina's face was getting hotter by the minute. "Dad," was all she could say.

Mum looked at her and said, "You know your Dad!"

Kat took another mouthful of the delicate red wine, looking across to them both.

"Okay! Spill everything, Dad," she said grinning.

Dad loved to gossip and told her as much as he knew, which was not a lot considering he was always talking to people all the time across the bar.

He told her that there were three brothers; Zach, Aaron and Craig he thought, but was not sure which name went with which person. The family had bought the Mountain Retreat homestead off Mr Harris who wanted to retire since his lovely wife had died. The cattle property was situated half way up a mountain range, about fifty kilometres from town and only accessible with four wheel drives; not the sort of place you would expect for three sexy-looking guys wanting to make a home. He seemed to think there was more to the story of the Williams family, but had no idea what it could be.

After a great dinner with her parents, Kat excused herself and went to her room. She had suddenly gone tired and threw on some sweat pants and a tee shirt and climbed into bed. After a long day travelling it wasn't long before she fell asleep.

The sunshine on her face was warming, as she walked along the windy path. The leaves dropping from the autumn trees were leaving an arrangement of amber and rust colours where she stepped. Katrina zipped up her coat, to stop the icy wind blowing through her clothes; her body seemed to be shaking with the cold. She stopped and looked around, where was she? This path way was all wrong. The leaves never dropped that shape or colour in Central Queensland and it did not look like her normal walking track. It was something she would see in Melbourne or England. She kept walking to see where it would go and heard a screech. She stopped and looked up to see a large bird of prey flying above her. It circled and came closer, she was sure she heard someone calling, *Katrina*. She looked up again and panicked, this bird was huge, looking similar to a wedge-tail eagle but at least four times bigger.

She started to run as fast as her legs would carry her down the path to get away, there was a loud screeching, a rush of feathers and Kat was grabbed from behind, huge talons came down each side of her head on to her shoulders she could hear her raincoat ripping as she was lifted into the sky. She screamed and woke up sweating and her heart beating out of her chest.

Chapter 2

With her heart still thumping in her chest, Kat grabbed a warm dressing gown from behind the bedroom door and went downstairs to find some water. Normally after drinking wine she would take a glass of water to bed with her, but last night she'd forgotten.

Kat grabbed a bottle of water out of the fridge in the bar and felt goose bumps crawling up her spine. She turned around to find one of the Williams brothers stood right behind her, she went to scream but he was quicker and in a flash had grabbed her around the waist, pulled her towards him and his lips found hers. She went to struggle but it was hopeless he was too strong. Her heart was racing again and she seemed shocked when her own arms encircled his beautiful strong neck and her body arched closer.

"This is not right, it cannot be happening!" her brain was yelling to her body, to STOP, but it wouldn't listen.

He pulled away only far enough to make sure she was not going to scream and keeping a firm hold on her waist, one of his hands started moving up and down her spine. She thought she was going to purr if he did not stop soon. This man's feel was heating up her body like it had not been heated in years.

"I am so sorry I frightened you, I only wanted to make sure you were okay! I heard you scream and I came to make sure you were all right, I was worried."

"What! Who are you? How dare you go around sneaking up on people and grabbing them? What do you mean you heard me scream? How could you hear me? I was sleeping in the staff wing on the other side of the building."

"I am sorry. I am Zach Williams and you are destined to be my mate. Of course I would hear you scream."

"Yes! Well I am not sure what this is all about, but I am nobody's girlfriend or mate. I don't think humans have mates. I think you mean, partners or wives and I am not yours and you are freaking me out!"

"I'll explain soon enough. Now let's get you back to bed."

He grabbed her hand and walked her back to the staff quarters.

After a rather disrupted sleep, Kat slept in until 9.30am. She grabbed a quick shower, dressed and headed downstairs.

"Good morning, sleepy head," her mother said when Kat walked into the kitchen. She grabbed a hug from her and went to find some food.

"There's some bacon in the oven, I can fry you a couple of eggs."

"Did you sleep all right?"

"Thanks, Mum, that would be great. I am starving for some reason, I had a bit of a restless night."

Kat put some bread in the toaster and went over to make some coffee.

She could feel her mother staring at her, with a look of worry on her face.

"Is everything all right, Katrina?"

"Just tired I guess!" Kat said.

"What's on today? You can make use of me until Tuesday, and then I promised I would visit Abbey," Kat said.

Mary smiled at her while dropping two eggs on a plate with some bacon for her and said, "Most of the guests are checking out this morning, so there are eight rooms to clean and with your help we should get through by lunch."

Katrina thought the cleaning and stripping beds would keep her busy, enough that she would not have to think about last night. If Zach was going today, maybe she would not find out what he meant about becoming his mate, he was really doing her head in.

When Zach walked Katrina back to her room last night he was deep in thought, saying nothing more and only stopping to kiss her on the lips gently before leaving and going back to his room.

Charlie came in and announced that the Williams brothers were checking out today, but Zach would be staying for another night. Something about a problem coming up and he needed to sort it out! Well that made her blush and she didn't know why, but her Dad noticed.

So maybe Kat was Zach's new problem. She sure wanted to be, until of course the holiday ended and the girls went back to Brisbane.

They cleaned and laundered all the rooms and came down for a late lunch, to find Charlie in the bar stocking the fridges, talking to Zach. Kat's heart starting beating fast in her chest, this guy was going to kill her with a heart attack for sure.

He looked up from his laptop towards the door as they walked in; it was the first time Kat had seen him smile. He was gorgeous with his dark wavy hair sitting on his shoulders, lighting up those dreamy hazily brown and golden eyes.

She hoped this guy wasn't psychic, because he would know what effect just his presence, was having on her. She just wanted to jump on to his lap and eat him. To her shock, he burst out laughing and with her face going redder, she dropped her plain green eyes and went to grab a drink from the bar trying to ignore him.

"You are funny," he said. Kat looked up to see both her parents checking Zach and her out.

To break the silence Kat asked what they were doing for lunch.

"Maybe Zach can join us, seeing as though he is all on his own!" Charlie said.

"Lovely, Dad match making already," she said and walked out to the kitchen to make some sandwiches.

Everyone sat and had lunch in the bar, while Katrina's father tried to find out more about what the Williams family were doing up at Thistle Ridge. Zach just changed the subject and asked about their only daughter. Mary and Charlie thought this was an easy topic and talked for nearly an hour about her. Everything down to life out there in Twin Hills when she was a child, when she grew up and left to go to boarding school.

Everything he wanted to know, they told him. It was like he was brainwashing her parents.

Kat was getting bored listening about herself; so she picked up the plates and took them back to the kitchen. When she returned they were agreeing about something and all looked up at her together.

"Zach has suggested that he take you out for a drive and show you the Harris property. Only if you want to?"

She was totally embarrassed that her father was still match making. Hadn't she only just arrived back home?

"Well that sounds good, Dad, but it's a bit late now. It will be dark in a few hours."

"Tomorrow is good if you like unless you have anything else planned," Zach said.

Zach caught her eyes and held them; she swore he was trying to read her mind or change it. Kat just shook her head as to imply nothing was happening.

"Don't you guys need me here tomorrow?"

"No, honey, you go and have fun. We will catch up the next day," said her mum.

"I have promised to go out to Abbey's place on Tuesday; I was going to help with some mustering, it's been years since I got on a horse."

He was still looking at her but his eyes had changed colour slightly and her senses could tell he was not happy about something.

Chapter 3

On Sunday morning Kat woke to sunshine coming in through her windows. The curtains had never been drawn shut; "That's strange, I always close them," she said to herself. Not worrying any more she took a shower and washed her uncontrollable auburn hair. It would not play nice, even after she blow dried it so she tied it back in a ponytail.

She had always wanted straight black hair like her mother's and not curly and unmanageable red hair like her father's.

"Maybe I could dye it, who was I kidding?"

She looked in the mirror and checked out her jeans; they needed an iron, after being screwed up in her case. But Kat was allergic to ironing so they went on creased; she grabbed a pale green wool jumper and applied a little make-up.

"This is the best I can do!" she said to no one in particular.

"God only knows what this incredibly mouth-watering, sexy guy sees in me!"

She walked into the kitchen to find her mum cooking some breakfast. After saying, "Good Morning!" she poured a coffee from the machine and sat down.

"Can you call your dad for breakfast, he's gone back in the dining room again."

Kat walked into the dining room to see their only guest sitting by himself finishing a coffee.

"Hi! I was looking for Charlie, he will miss breakfast if he does not hurry up."

"Good morning, Katrina, you look lovely, that green jumper really brings out the colour of your eyes. You should wear it all the time!"

She could feel the heat claiming her face. *Who says that?* she thought to herself. He smiled and laughed at her.

"I saw your father when he brought my breakfast in but I don't know where he is now!"

"Okay, thanks. Please call me Kat! Katrina is so old fashioned."

"I like it, I think it suits you."

Her whole body was starting to react to the intense and smouldering look in his eyes; they seemed to be pulling her across the room. The next thing she was aware of, she was touching his face with her fingers, rubbing them up and down his cheek. She was standing at his dining table, not remembering even walking there. She suddenly heard her mother calling her and Zach dropped eye contact and released her from his spell.

Shaking her head, she went in search of her father, and found him in the bar polishing glasses.

"Come on! Mum's yelling it's breakfast time. You know how she hates it when we don't come!"

With that, Dad grabbed her around the shoulders and they marched back to the kitchen.

Today Kat was going for a drive with Zach, was it a date? She wasn't sure. She was looking forward to seeing the Harris's place, since she had only been out there as a child. She was a little nervous being all alone with Zach; it had been a long time since she had been on any dates. It was a little intimidating because he was so good looking, smart and she felt plain and boring beside him.

She just could not see what he was thinking about when he looked at her.

After breakfast she went to find him, in the dining room. He was not there so she went upstairs and knocked on his bedroom door. He opened the door and grabbed her into strong embrace, Kat looked up and he found her lips.

This guy knew how to melt a girl, she wondered if he did this all the time with his girlfriends, because a sexy guy like this would have to have a few hiding somewhere.

"No girlfriends," he said. She looked up into his eyes and waited for more conversation but nothing else came.

He took her hand and led her back downstairs where she found her coat on the hook by the front door. Her father was in the bar and called out, "See ya later guys, have a good one."

"See ya later, Dad; don't know when I will be back," and shut the front door.

Zach's gold BMW was parked outside, he opened the door for her but instead of climbing in she looked over her shoulder at him. Suddenly feeling panicked she asked, "Am I going to be safe with you? Will you bring me back?"

He reached over and grabbed the lapels of her coat and turned her body around to face him, then he pulled her as close to his chest as possible. She could feel his heart beating and when he looked at her his eyes were glowing gold. She swallowed, knowing what a rabbit looked like before a dingo attacked it for a meal.

"Yes! No! And yes!" She rolled her emerald eyes, still looking at him and started to chew the inside of her lip; she had no idea what this guy was saying.

"Yes, I will bring you back only because I like your parents. No I don't want to, I want nothing better than to keep you prisoner in my own bed, where I can make love to you all day and all night."

She swallowed hard wondering what that would be like and if it would ever get to that.

"And yes, you are very safe, maybe not this beautiful body but I would never hurt you, you mean too much to me." *Wow did he just say my body was beautiful! I always thought my small frame was inadequate wanting to be taller, instead of my 5ft 3 inches.*

"Stop interrupting me with your thoughts!" Zach said. "Katrina, I know we have only just met, but as soon as I saw you I knew you were mine to protect, and claim. Come on let me show you Thistle Ridge, and we can talk more."

He kissed her slowly and then walked around to the driver's side and started the car; her body was still shaking from the declaration he had just given her. Sitting there next to him she was thinking she was totally screwed.

They drove for about half an hour stopping only for the odd kangaroo wanting to cross the road. At the bottom of the mountain range, their property started and Zach stopped to put the hub caps in and turn the car over to four-wheel drive. They climbed up the sharp dirt road through the mountain pass, up a rocky terrain and turned in to a long driveway of large ghost gums standing tall. The trees were magnificent; the white trunks were so wide across their girths, three people hugging them would not be enough to get around them.

"They must be hundreds of years old," said Kat.

She looked up at him and smiled, he must be reading her mind.

"Can you read minds?" she asked.

She should have been more freaked out that he knew her thoughts, or maybe she was getting used to this weird crap.

"They must have been here way before Mr Harris, or maybe Mr Harris's parents planted them?" she said.

"I think the previous owners planted them, or so the real estate told us," Zach said.

They kept travelling to the end of the drive until they reached a huge homestead. It was not unlike the normal Australian homestead with the wide wraparound verandas, surrounded by more gum trees but from the main building it went off in four different directions, similar to a cross.

When Katrina looked through the bottlebrush trees surrounding the homestead, there were smaller timber cabins placed in hideaway spots, with all their chimneys smoking. She thought to herself that there was more than one family living up here!

Zach pulled up and jumped out of the car, before she knew it, he was at her door pulling her out. He grabbed Kat around the waist and they walked towards the main building. They were met on the veranda by his two brothers, Aaron and Craig, whom she had only seen from a distance, in the dining room and then one of them was growling, or she thought it had been one of them. They both greeted her, welcoming her to their home, and shook her hand. It was nice to put their names to their faces, at least she knew more than her father now.

"I brought Katrina for a visit and to spend some time with her, away from prying eyes at the hotel. I thought I would take her for a ride up the ridge, to show her the place."

They both nodded and then asked if they should come, and accompany them. He told them he was good and would see them at lunch. *Why would they want to come with us?* she thought. There were so many questions she wanted to ask.

Zach took her into his new home, and gave her a guided tour, stopping at the kitchen to introduce Kat to his mother, Amy.

"Hello, Katrina, welcome to our home." Katrina looked at her and smiled.

Amy had the same dark nearly black wavy hair all the boys had and bright blue eyes that were dazzling. Katrina kept smiling and went towards her to shake her hand, but instead was grabbed and hugged. She could feel her face going red again; *I don't know why I was embarrassed. She seems very nice,* she thought.

"Come on let's see where the boss is! And then we can leave."

Zach's father came out of one of the new extensions. "I thought I heard you two walk in."

"Father, this is Katrina."

"Nice to meet you, Katrina."

"Katrina, this is Richard," as he took her hand to shake it.

"Hi Richard pleased to meet you, you have a lovely home here and please call me Kat!"

Zach smiled but made no comment. Zach's father was very tall and proud looking; his movements were very graceful, she wondered if he had ever been a dancer. Standing tall at around 6ft 5inches at least, he was taller than all his sons and his eyes were the strangest deep rusty gold she had ever seen. She was thinking maybe contacts and then Kat thought about seeing Zach's eyes change colour, knowing they were probably real.

Zach took Katrina's hand and took her for a quick tour through their new home; it was very regal, lots of reds and golds in the satins of the furnishings and heavy curtains. There was plenty of natural timber used inside which gave it a log cabin idea, only on a much larger and elaborate scale.

There was a huge stone fire place roaring away with sandal-wood logs that took up the main feature wall in the lounge and the smell from the timber was soothing.

The four new extensions added on from when Mr Harris lived here had been designed to accommodate a private area for each of them with separate living quarters. Zach took Katrina through to his private rooms and they were surprisingly spacious. The first room they entered was a large sitting room, to the right a large bay window, with a built-in cushioned seat letting in the morning's sunshine and off to the left side another room for an office. The natural beiges and golds used to furnish these rooms continued into the large bedroom with a king size timber four poster bed and an *en-suite*. It was large, there were two vanity basins, a large corner bath, a double shower and in another room, a toilet. This room was all fitted out in black marble and gold trimmings for the taps, hand rails and towel rails. Gold coloured towels and gold rugs on the floors.

"You really like gold, don't you?"

He smiled not answering back and pulled her towards him, she was starting to like the way her body felt in his strong arms. He bent his head down and kissed her gently, her arms reached up and her delicate fingers gripped his soft hair before pulling his head down closer to her face. Kat could not get enough of him, her body was pulsating, his hands moved from her back to her waist line and they started sliding up under the green jumper. Zach's hands were warm and strong, as he lightly pressed his fingertips along her rib cage; the electrical sensation running over her skin was breathtaking. She gasped for air pulling, back from their kiss, looking back into his eyes. The intense golds had changed and they were now glowing a deep bronze.

That was very different, but the effect of his eyes covered Kat's body in goose bumps, and her nipples were standing up.

He pulled away and looked at her, bronze eyes now changed back to his normal hazel colour.

"If we don't get moving, my next move will be to drag you over there."

Indicating the bed with his eyes. She was so tempted right then to let him, but Kat had only known him a couple of days and his whole family were just down the hall.

"Come on then, show me what you have got!"

Laughing, he grabbed her hand and they walked back outside.

They took a quad bike out of the shed and he let her get up first before he climbed on. When his thighs touched hers, she felt a hot flush to her face and body. As he sat down he pushed her legs apart and she was instantly aware of his strong muscular back and lower region. It was very cosy, almost too cosy. Her mind was flooded with naughty thoughts; she was sure she heard him laugh but was unsure with the noise of the bike.

They took off up through the forest of yellow wattle trees, the bottlebrushes were a picture too, white and red brush flowers. It was so pretty and very quiet here you could think it was another world; the city noise was one thing she did not miss.

They reached the top of a ridge and an excellent lookout spot and turned the quad bike off; Zach climbed down and turned around to help Katrina get off. He held her around the waist and then kissed her, it was a slow kiss, not heated but it was still making her body react.

They stood in a small clearing of stumpy brown grass and large rocks, surrounded by ghost gums and large flame trees in full blossom. It was breathtaking, looking out across the views they could see for miles.

"This is the eastern ridge and it looks down the front side of the property, you can see the house over there, to the left."

Kat looked but could not see a house. Her eyesight was lacking X-ray vision or something. All she spotted was two kookaburras in the trees about two hundred metres away, laughing at them.

"Sorry, I can't see that far. Maybe I need to be looking through your eyes. Okay! I have a few questions!"

"I thought you might!" he said smiling.

"Okay, first question. I want to know how you read my thoughts, can you read minds? Can you read everyone's mind? Why your eyes change colour with your different moods and the mate thing? You know I am only here for two weeks then I go back to Brisbane!"

He walked over to the bike and pulled out a thick blanket and sat it down on a large rock. Then he walked back and found water and a flask of hot coffee. He poured two mugs of steaming hot coffee while she sat and waited. He passed her one with a spoon and some sugar, and after giving him back the spoon and sugar Zach sat down close to her on the rock.

"Let's start at the beginning, without all the freaky details, as I am not ready to lose you yet."

"I can read minds. It's just something I have always been able to do – and not just your mind. I can read everyone's. My brothers get really pissed when they are trying to hide something, especially around someone's birthday, or when one of them had a hot date. It's quite funny; they have to bribe me to keep quiet."

"What I am discussing with you, we don't normally share with humans. Humans don't know we exist and it's only that the higher authorities above have chosen you to become my mate," he said pointing up to the sky.

"Some things you will find out today. Other questions, for your own safety, will have to wait until another day."

"What you do with your eyes is almost hypnotic. Did you do something to me in the dining room?"

"The eyes changing colour is part of what I am and which I cannot go into a lot, but yes, I can use them that way. I would never use them to hurt you, to make you do bad things, for example rob a bank. Only possibly to seduce you."

"Wait, have you been in my bedroom?" His grin was alarming.

Kat could feel the heat radiating off him. He was really enjoying this.

"Not in your bedroom exactly," he said still grinning.

"Explain why you keep calling me your mate?"

"We are shifters and only get one chance to find our real mate. We can have steady girlfriends that are not our true mates, but if our mate walked in to the same room that we were in, the girlfriend would no longer stand a chance. The mate would take the love of his or her mate firstly and never look back. They would be committed to that one person for all time. There would be no breakup and no divorce, it would remain for ever, and no one could ever come between them.

"Once committed to that relationship, they would never be parted from each other. You do need to know that after I claim you, you will never be the same again. My soul will be tied to your soul for ever and you will be connected to me. You will be loved and protected by myself and my family and no harm will ever come to you or your family."

"It's a lot to take in, Zach. So what you're saying is if I don't want a relationship with you then you will never find another true mate."

"That's correct, but don't let that be the only reason to do this!"

"Well there's no rush. I can tell you now I was not looking for something serious in a relationship. I have my job and I love my freedom and living in the city. That's why I left home, as soon as I could; I couldn't wait to get out of here," Katrina said looking at him.

"I only need you to think about it."

"I will. I am off to Abbey's in a few days, and the break from us will give me time to think this over."

"I don't really like you going there by yourself. I don't want you riding those stupid horses; won't you rethink the whole idea?"

"No, I came on holiday to visit my family and her family. I have been doing this sort of thing all my life and I have not ridden a horse in over twelve months."

"Will you take a satellite phone with you? And then you can call me if you need to! I really wish you would change your mind."

"If it will make you happier, then I will take the phone. I don't want to upset you, it's just my mind is made up."

"You are so stubborn, my lovely little human," he said and kissed her. "Come on let's finish the tour."

They arrived back at the house two hours later and parked the quad bike in the shed. Zach took Kat's hand and they walked back across the lawn. They could hear talking and someone was cooking onions. The smell was divine and made her stomach growl.

"I hope that growling is your stomach!"

"Hey that reminds me, do you guys growl? I swear I heard someone growl in the bar the other night."

"Possibly, that might have been me. I am sorry, I didn't realise what the time was."

"Oh! It's all right," she said and went to touch his cheek, for some reason she thought he needed reas-suring. He was really trying too hard to make her happy and he could have anyone.

Zach took her hand and held it giving her a stern look. "You really don't know how lovely you are, do you?"

She just smiled and said, "No one's ever told me that. Oh! Except my parents, but they're biased."

"Come on, I think they are waiting for us!" So they followed their noses to the barbeque, the smell was coming from the back veranda.

They found a large party in full swing with Zach's family and twenty or more of their friends. Kat could not count them all.

Feeling self-conscious, she hid behind Zach. He must have felt her slow down to a stop. He stopped, hugged her to his side and walked up the steps towards everyone.

Richard held up a hand with a glass of red wine for her, feeling nervous she took it and thanked him, and took a mouthful while Zach grabbed a beer from the icebox beside the table.

Richard spoke and the whole room went still, he seemed to be generating some power over the whole group. She noticed even the birds had shut up.

"I'd like everyone to join in and welcome Zach's new girlfriend Katrina to Thistle Ridge. Her parents, some of you already know, are the owners of Twin Hill's hotel in town.

"Others will get to meet them later, I am sure, especially as they have the best accommodation for miles around and I can see us having a few functions here at Thistle Ridge."

Everyone on the veranda held glasses or beers high and toasted, "To Katrina. Welcome to Thistle Ridge."

She was so embarrassed, feeling her face grow hotter and hotter. After the toast the guests mingled and introduced themselves to her. A lot of them seemed to be excited to meet her, and she was unsure why. Zach kept touching her on the back or around the waist but never left her side. Feeling him close to her, she started to relax and enjoy herself. One couple, Louise and Brian had bought the supermarket last year and another couple, Suzette and James had bought the post office/bank.

Kat was amazed she had missed that news, maybe her mum or dad had told her at some time and she had forgotten, but she was starting to think there was a little more to the story.

When the food was laid out, everyone stopped talking and dug into the tucker. It was a good barbeque with lots of different cuts of steak, good old sausages and rissoles and heaps of yummy salads. Zach's parents had really put on a good spread.

As the meal finished Zach excused them from the party and took her back to his private living room. He threw some more logs on the fire and turned around to look at her.

"Well I am glad that's all over! I am so sorry about that, I didn't know they were planning a large get together."

"It's all right it's not your fault, Zach."

She walked into his open arms for the strong embrace he was offering. He kissed her lightly on the lips and then pushed his tongue into her mouth, opening it wider it was lighting up all her senses. She pushed her tongue back into his mouth and then felt Zach's hands moving down her arms to her legs, before she knew it Zach had picked her up and carried her over to the couch and laid her down. He lay down beside her and grabbed the throw rug off the arm rest to keep them both warm, although the fire was doing a good job at that.

"I would have preferred to get to know your family first. I don't know why some of the guests were so excited to meet me, haven't you ever had girlfriends before?"

"Yes of course, did you think I was a monk? I have dated lots of girls but not in the same sense, this is very different! You will find out soon enough!"

Chapter 4

After Kat's afternoon with Zach, her brain was in overload. She could not stop thinking what he had been telling her. The thing that was getting to her most of all was that he had told her he was not a monk. Zach had, had plenty of girlfriends, unlike her who had only ever had two boyfriends. She didn't know why it bothered her as much as it did but it certainly annoyed her. Kat did not like the idea of sharing him with anyone and didn't know how she'd react if later had to meet one of them.

She woke early after a very restless night, to find her curtains drawn back again and the sunshine lighting up her room. What was she doing in the middle of the night? Was Zach doing something to her? Shaking her head, she climbed out of bed and headed for a shower. Hoping it would bring life to her tired, aching body.

The kitchen was a hive of activity, both her parents were doing tasks; her father cooking breakfast, while her mother was rolling out pastry.

"Morning. What's going on in here?"

"We have a luncheon party booked in today for the town council members. They have decided to have it here. They have always organised their meetings in Charters Towers but out of the blue they called us."

"Well that's good, more income for you. What can I do?"

"You could peel some carrots and then some potatoes. I am going to give them roast chicken and roast beef, roast potatoes, glazed carrots and green beans."

"Yummy."

"I am also making blueberry pies, an apple tart and black forest gateau for desserts."

"Why didn't you wake me?"

"Oh honey, it's all right. We have plenty of time," said her mum

"Okay! Let's stop for breakfast," her dad said as Zach walked into the kitchen.

"I have put six tables together in the dining room and added fifteen chairs around them. All I need now is cutlery and napkins."

"That's great, Zach, thanks for that."

"Good morning, sleepy head," Zach said as he walked around the work bench and kissed Katrina on the lips.

Dad was grinning from ear to ear at Zach's actions.

"So you guys had a good day yesterday?" Katrina's face a little pink, she smiled at her dad and said, "Yes it was very nice. I met Zach's family and some of their friends. Zach took me for a tour around the farm on a quad bike and then we joined in his parents' party for a barbeque lunch."

"Well that would have been nice. I expect the property has changed a little since we were out there," said Mary.

They sat in the dining room and ate their breakfast while Zach told Katrina's parents all about the renovating they were doing and had already achieved.

At half past eleven, the council members started arriving at the hotel for their meeting. Charlie went straight to the bar to meet them and serve any drinks that were needed.

Zach went and floated in the bar, just in case he was needed to help Charlie.

"Zach's very helpful, isn't he, and so good looking?" Mary said.

"Mum! Yes, he's pretty talented with those hands and also very good looking. I love his hazel eyes."

Katrina thinking to herself that he was probably listening to them, from the dining room. She said, "I still don't get what he sees in me. You know I am just plain looking and not a sexy, tall skinny blonde model. This is what I would expect him to be chasing."

"Katrina, stop that silly nonsense. You are gorgeous and stop thinking you are not. I would give anything to have those beautiful green eyes. Your hair is lovely too, it might be a handful, but it's a dark auburn. You are lucky it's not red, and then I could understand your problems."

Katrina threw on a hotel uniform and helped her mother take out the meals. She was surprised to see Zach's father there involved in the council. She thought they had only been in this area a few months.

He stood up to meet her and gave her a hug.

"Hello! It's nice to see you again, Katrina."

"Hello, Richard. This is my mother, Mary Cross."

"Pleased to meet you."

He took Mary's hand and shook it. She seemed to be a little nervous and dropped her eyes. They continued to bring out the meals until everyone was served. After the desserts and coffee had been given out, Mary and Katrina retreated back to the kitchen to clear up.

"Well, that's a real surprise!"

"What's that Mum?"

"I didn't realize your Zach Williams was related to Richard Williams. I used to know him years ago, it's a small world. I have not seen Richard since we were both at college."

"Did he recognize you?"

"No, I don't think so; it was a long time ago."

"Well maybe you can get together after the meeting."

"Maybe," she said and started to wash up in deep thought. Katrina watched her for a while, wondering if anything was wrong with her mother.

The hotel continued to be busy throughout the day, with tourists arriving for their overnight stays. They were the only place in town for accommodation and to find cooked meals, so it was a full-time job keeping up. Hailey worked for them, mostly cooking at lunch times and some evenings, but sometimes they could have done with even more help.

Zach helped with the rush and then disappeared upstairs to make some phone calls. He was leaving in the morning for Thistle Ridge.

The next morning came too soon, and after dressing in some old jeans Katrina pulled out an overnight bag from her wardrobe and packed some more jeans, tee shirts, sweats and undies for a few days' mustering. She decided she could always wash her clothes at Abbey's if she decided to stay any longer and she really didn't know what she wanted to do, especially after last night. Zach had spent the rest of the evening with her, just talking and kissing and cuddling in the bar. They had stayed up after the bar closed and all the guests and locals left. She was enjoying being with him, but she was still not sure she could give up her life in the city.

She knew her parents would love the chance to get her back home. But was she ready?

Charlie gave Katrina a lift out to Abbey's parents' station, after breakfast was finished with and she had said goodbye to Zach. Kat sure missed her little car, which was in Brisbane, for a runaround, but it was a city car and would not survive on these dirt roads.

There were large grey and red kangaroos out in the central highlands and all through the west. Some of the big males could reach over six foot in height and heavy but none of them were road smart. If she had the misfortune of hitting a large grey kangaroo it would wipe her car out; kangaroos normally hit the bonnet and pushed the radiator in. Sometimes they could end up on the windscreen, smashing it to pieces and pushing in the cab. Anyway it was not a good idea and it gave her a good opportunity to ask her father about the guests at the barbeque.

"Hey Dad, I met Louise and Brian, the new owners of the supermarket, yesterday out at Zach's place. I can't remember you telling me the Smyths sold the supermarket and moved away."

"Yes, it was all very sudden. One day they were talking about adding on a new cold room and the next thing they were leaving town. They could not get out of here fast enough, it was very strange. Louise and Brian seem very nice, they work long hours at the supermarket and are pretty private people. They have come here a couple of times for dinner but don't socialise that much. I am surprised they were out at Zach's."

"I also met Suzette and James, who bought the post office. Did you tell me about them coming?"

"I am sure I told you about them, maybe I didn't."

Dad seemed to be unsure whether he had told Katrina or not.

"So what happened?"

"James and Suzette came out to Twin Hills whilst they were touring around Queensland. They fell in love with the place and offered the owners of the post office a huge amount of money to take over the business and once the two of them were trained for the post service and the bank, the old owners left town as well. It's really very strange! It was almost like they had been scared for their lives or something."

They were both quiet as Dad turned into Abbey's property off the main highway. She'd always thought it was strange they never had any farm dogs to bark when visitors arrived.

Abbey had told her her mother, Eileen, did not like dogs for some reason and that she preferred the geese as watch dogs. She would have had anything rather than geese; Kat remembered they had always chased her as a child.

Abbey's parents and her brothers, lived on this large cattle and cotton property, ten kilometres out of town, they had over three thousand acres, which was divided into smaller areas to grow cotton, sunflowers and fatten cattle. Abbey and Kat had grown up together from day one as their mothers were best friends. They had been home-schooled, together with Abbey's brothers, Jared and Abbey's twin, Andy; and when it was time to go to high school the three of them followed Jared who was one year older, to All Souls boarding school in Charters Towers. They were all mates growing up and never really argued. Jared and Andy treated her just like a sister and when they first went to Brisbane came to visit as often as they could to make sure they were safe and happy. It was really sweet and she loved them all.

The front door opened and Jared and Abbey came running out. Jared picked Kat up and swung her around and kissed her cheek.

"It's good to see you, kiddo! It's been far too long," Jared said.

"Thanks, Jared" Kat said still in his tight embrace.

"God, you even smell different, what's that smell?"

She punched him, thinking he was being rude about her perfume, but noticed him exchange a quick look with Abbey.

They waved goodbye to her dad, who wanted to keep going, and then went inside the house. It was good to see Abbey's parents again, after so long she had really missed them all. Eileen and John had been her extended family for so long and after lots of greeting hugs they all pulled up chairs around the kitchen table for a welcomed coffee.

Andy came in from working in the stables and pulled Kat out of her chair for a big hug and then went over to grab some coffee as well.

"So, Kat what have you been up to, anything exciting at the hotel since you got here?" asked Abbey.

"Well, I know this is really strange and it was quite weird to start with, but I met someone. It was a guest who was staying at the hotel with his brothers. The three of them had been waiting for a road train delivery or something. He's called Zach Williams and he's bought the Harris's property with his family."

All the room went quiet and seemed in shock whilst she was talking.

"He seems really nice and he invited me out to the property on Sunday."

"Did you meet his father? And what did you make of him, Katrina?" John asked.

"He came over very regal and there was something wrong with his eyes, they were the most beautiful colour I have ever seen, like rusty gold. I think they must have been contacts, because no one has eyes that colour. Ah!"

They were all looking at each other; it was starting to unnerve her.

"What?" she whispered at them. The room was still quiet and she asked again. "What's wrong, what did I say? You'd better tell me, is there something I need to know? Because you guys are looking at me like I have the plague or worse."

"Did Zach say anything that you thought was weird, Kat?" Jared asked, looking worried.

"Yeah, he kept telling me I was his mate and I told him I was no one's mate, or puppy dog for that matter."

They all laughed but there was something wrong.

"You guys need to tell me if he's some kind of weirdo because I will stop seeing him. It's only until I go back to Brisbane surely he cannot be serious about a relationship, I told him I was only here for two weeks."

Eileen looked up and said very quietly, "The poor darling's in trouble. She needs to know, John!"

"Please, guys, you need to tell me!"

Kat was really starting to think that her day could not get any worse, and then it did.

"Kat, did he say anything about wanting to claim you?" Andy asked.

"Yes he told me that if he claimed me my life would be tied to his for ever, no separation and no divorce. He also told me that I was a human and that he'd let me into a secret world that humans don't normally know about."

46

John looked at her and said, "Okay! Katrina, you need to listen very carefully and what we tell you would be best kept here and not repeated. Can you understand what we are saying, honey? We really don't need to get your parents involved if we can help it. Not until we know what's really happening with you and Zach."

"First of all, the family that bought the Harris's property are shape shifters. That means they are half human and half animal. Also, you need to know that they are from a long line of royal families," Jared said.

"Zach's parents are very rare in the shifter world, Richard is a lion shifter and I have only met one other in my life and he lives in France, hidden away in a large castle," John said.

"The lion shifter was supposed to be the first shifter developed when Mother Nature was messing around all those hundreds or thousands of years ago. They follow the same path as the large African cat does and are top of any food chain. The Lion shifter is higher than any wolf, bear, tiger, puma shifter etc., and they are supposed to be able to manipulate other shifters or human being, with his or her power and radiate energy from around them, using elements," he said.

"Oh! That explains a lot. When Richard spoke at the barbeque yesterday every one fell silent, even the crows outside in the trees shut up and they never do. There was a sort of an electric current pulsating in the room, but not if you know what I mean. It was weird!" Kat explained.

"His wife is regal in her own right as an eagle shifter; she is the largest and most feared of all birds of prey, to all shape shifters and to other birds. She is a wedge-tailed eagle," John said.

Kat was suddenly thinking of my dream; and felt the blood drain from her head and her stomach turn over. She was going to be sick.

"Kat are you all right?"

"No I think I am going to be sick."

She ran to the down stairs bathroom and brought up her breakfast. After a while she came back out feeling a little better. Kat took the toothbrush Abbey was holding and returned to the bathroom to clean her teeth.

The talking stopped when she walked back into the kitchen and sat down. Eileen gave her a glass of water and some Panadol for the headache she now had, and an ice pack for the back of her neck.

"Sorry about that honey, I was not trying to scare you!" John said.

"It's okay John. I was remembering the dream I had after the first night I met Zach. I was walking down a path somewhere on my own and it was autumn because the leaves were falling off the trees. Only the leaves weren't from around here, more like down south near Melbourne. Anyway, suddenly I hear this screeching and I turned around to see this huge eagle thing in the sky and it swooped down and grabbed me by my shoulders, the next thing I knew I woke up screaming."

"What happened then?" asked Eileen.

"I went down to the bar to get a bottle of water out of the fridge and Zach came to find me and asked me if I was all right. He told me he had heard me scream."

"I asked him how he could hear me when I am on the other side of the hotel away from all guests."

No one said any more until John spoke again, looking very worried.

"What you are looking at is that Zach is a shifter. What he is we are not sure about as we have not met

48

him. Normally they follow their parents' bloodline. So I would think he's either lion or eagle, so he's rare. If he intends to claim you as his true mate, there is nothing you can do but accept."

"Or I can go back to Brisbane, forget this ever happened and let him find someone else."

"Maybe he is something else," Jared said.

"No way! Jared. That's only ever been written about in books and it's myth not real," said Andy.

"Says you guys talking about shifters! Jared, what do you think he is?" Katrina asked.

"I don't want to scare you any more than you are now, so I will keep it to myself."

Looking around the room she was suddenly intrigued as to how this whole family she had known all her life were telling her something that they all knew a lot about. They seemed to sense the same thing as they all looked at each other waiting for someone to speak.

"John, you need to tell me! Everything!" she said.

"We might need some more coffee," said Eileen as she walked back over to the coffee machine to refill all the cups.

"We are shifters, too, Katrina. We belong to the Haliaeetus Lecucogaster family, for similar explanation we are members of the Eagle family, we are White Bellied Sea Eagles. Now before you ask we came out here twenty-five years ago, to get away from the coast for privacy. It was getting very built up where we lived and someone would have ended up seeing us, as we liked to fish at night."

"We built three very large dams, stocked with thousands of fish. We have also the fresh water creeks coming off the mountains full of perch and in the summer season, barramundi. So we can fish as much as we like, when we transform and without worrying about who will see us," John said.

"How come I have never seen any of you doing these things, I grew up here?" Kat asked.

"You have on occasions but shrugged it off when someone said you were imaging it," Abbey said.

"So you have been lying to me my whole life?" Katrina said, looking around the room at the five faces she loved and cared about.

"No, honey we were protecting you. How would we have coped if you went back to your parents and said something? It makes people jumpy and they start to panic for no reason," John said.

"We also love you; you became part of our family so it was easier to say you must have imagined it. So in the end we could stay here and love the people around us, meaning you and your family," Eileen said.

"So will you show me, later? Oh! How stupid I am!!! That explains why Abbey suggested flying home. She's got her own wings!"

"Yes, we will, it will be nice to let you in on our secret at long last. And Abbey, that's mean because you know Katrina hasn't got wings!" said John.

"Oh! Dad! I was just having a go!" said Abbey.

"Is there something happening in the town?" Katrina asked.

"What do you mean?" John asked.

"Well, Dad could not remember telling me that there were new people coming into town, buying up the businesses."

"They are all shifters, Katrina!"

"Are my parents safe to be left here in this town? What about the rest of the local population that have lived here all their lives?"

"Of course they are, nothing changes and being told will only freak them out. If shifters are moving into this area because they are safer here, away from city populations, why would they want to cause any problems? All we want to do is live in peace with humans."

That afternoon they took the Land Cruiser down to the first dam, about ten kilometres away from the main house, in a covered area of ghost gums and tee trees. They all got out and Kat watched as the coats came off and then the guys stripped off their shirts.

"Wow, you didn't tell me I got to see you two naked!"

"Andy, you can slap her you're closest!" Jared yelled out.

"This is all you are seeing, sweet pea," said Andy.

She laughed and sat back on the bumper bar of the Cruiser, taking in the show. The boys had really filled out since they were all teenagers; both had strong shoulders and hard chests. There arms were huge, with muscles bulging. She wondered if they would have the same problems trying to find their true mates, especially stuck out here away from everything.

Abbey and her mother had stripped down to tee shirts, with very low backs. Handy if you had to make room for wings and watching them transform was going to be amazing. One minute there were five normal people standing around her and the next, they all started to shimmer. She tried to see what was happening but the glow around them was too intense. One second she saw pairs of white wings extending out from behind them all, the next there was a lot of feathers instead of skin. John, Eileen and Andy had already shifted into these giant birds of prey hoovering in front of her.

"O M G."

"That's brilliant. Hold it, Abbey let me look can I feel them?"

When Abbey turned around, Kat had noticed her eyes had gone completely black. *No colour or white left it's freaky but a good freaky,* Kat thought as she jumped down off the car and went to touch Abbey's wings, they were so soft. All their wings were a very pale grey, with softer white feathers underneath and brown tips going back where their tail feathers would be later. Jared and Abbey finished shifting when they could see Katrina was not going to freak out, screaming or something worse.

The five giant birds all took off, leaving a rush of cold wind behind them, it was incredible. Why had they waited so long to tell her, she could not believe this was happening? She actually wished she was up there too. There was a loud screech more like a goose honking noise and they all flew in formation. Now she knew why they liked geese so much, they really sounded like them.

They flew around until the sun went down, and then they started to hunt. Jared plunged to the water below and extended his yellow feet with large black talons. He hit the water fast and came up with a huge fish in his talons, she was wondering what he was going to do with this fish, when he flew above her and dropped the fish right at her feet. She was sure he was laughing when the live fish hit the ground, flapping and leaving her to squeal.

"Not funny Jared!" she yelled out.

He was still laughing when he flew down to take care of it.

"That was amazing, Jared, the way you caught that fish, it looked so natural."

Jared retracted his wings and went down to the water's edge to clean the fish. He changed his left hand to talons and ripped up the stomach of the fish, pulled out the guts and then brought it back nice and clean and through it into the ice box.

That night they sat down to dinner, eating freshly cooked fish, homemade bread straight from the oven and a garden salad. The conversation around the dinner table was all about the cattle and what everyone's jobs were going to be during the next week. There was no more talk about shifters, which was a relief to Katrina.

Her head was already in turmoil thinking about Zach, his family and now the family she had grown up with, never knowing this life existed and being so close to it all her own life, without the slightest idea.

However, Abbey was itching to get Katrina on her own so she could ask more questions. When the girls left the others to get ready for bed, she could see Abbey really had not given up on the subject of Zach.

"So, Kat, please tell me what does he look like? Is he covered in muscles and tattoos?"

Kat was laughing at her best friend. "He's lovely."

"Not funny, Kat, tell me the details?"

"Okay! He's got dark wavy hair nearly down to his shoulders and beautiful hazel eyes. That change colour when he is worried or trying to seduce me. He has large biceps and muscle everywhere to make a girl drool. He's got to be close to six foot in height with large broad shoulders and a strong back that should carry me any where and a really nice, firm, muscular behind. I have not seen him naked, or without a shirt so I don't know if he has any tattoos. So I will have to let you know when and if we get that far."

"Hey hang on a minute. Did you tell Dad about Zach's eyes?"

"No! Why?"

"No reason. What about his brothers, are they the same, good looking?"

"You know, if you had come in to the bar with me the other night you would have been able to goggle at them yourself."

"Yes, I know. Now I am kicking myself."

"Well the two brothers are just as yummy looking and they all have the same dark wavy hair. Only Zach has hazel eyes and the other two brothers have blue. When I say blue, I mean like a real electric blue. They seem to pull you in like the sea."

"Wow, now I am really kicking myself. Do they have girlfriends?"

"I don't know but I can ask Zach next time we catch up."

"So they all live under one roof with their parents, I think that would be strange."

"No, it works quite well. They have designed the house so it splits up into four, similar to a huge criss-cross. So the three brothers and their parents have separate living quarters away from each other. The house is great; you will have to visit it. I went through to Zach's rooms and they were furnished beautifully. In the bathroom, black marble and gold trims. Big fire place in the lounge with a bay window.

"Does he have a bed?" asked Abbey.

"Yes he does Abbey and it's a king size and no, I have not tried it out," she said laughing.

"I think I will go for a quick shower now. All of a sudden I need to cool myself down," cried Abbey.

She walked off to the bathroom, leaving Katrina laughing.

In the morning the girls were woken up by Jared. "Come on you pair of slack asses, get your selves out of bed."

"Lovely, now I remember why I missed you so much, Jared," Kat said.

"Yes, he makes me want to punch him like when we were kids," said Abbey.

They both climbed out of bed and after dressing dragged themselves downstairs. They managed to find the coffee and drink some before the guys came in and pinched it all. Eileen was cooking scrambled eggs with onion and bacon, it smelt divine.

"Can we help with anything?" Kat asked.

"No, dear, it's all ready, just have a seat and start eating before the noisy ones come in."

John, Andy and Jared came in and Eileen was right, they were full on chatting and making a real din.

"You two girls really aren't morning people, are you?" Andy said.

"Shut up," they both called out at the same time. Then the kitchen turned into a big teasing session during breakfast.

They were heading out to Stoney Creek, which was roughly a good hour's drive from the main house yards. It was where the second lot of cattle yards were on the property and where the stock were brought in to check, dip, sometimes castrate and separate the older steers for market.

Abbey and Kat were towing one horse float with two horses in it, Andy and Jared in the horse truck with another six horses and John following up the rear with all the camping supplies. The shed had bunks to sleep on, a small kitchen, a shower outside and toilet so it was more comfortable than sleeping in tents.

Katrina's new satellite phone rang in her bag and made them both jump!

"Sorry I had forgotten about that."

"Hello!"

"Hello Katrina, how is everything going? I miss you already."

"It's only been one day and a night. How are you going to be after a week?"

"Do you really need to stay that long? I could come and get you, take you somewhere where we could be alone, just you and me?"

"That's so tempting, but I promised Abbey I would spend a few days with her, you can understand that."

"He can always come out and help, and then I can meet this guy who's stolen your heart," interrupted Abbey.

"Abbey, shut up." She was laughing so loud she could not hear what Jared was saying on the two ways.

Abbey picked up the two way, "Yes Jared what is it? I know that, do I look stupid," and started to argue with him.

"Who's Jared, Katrina?"

"He's my big brother. Well Abbey's brother really, but they adopted me from a young age into their family as Mum and Dad were always so busy with the hotel. I have spent a lot of my childhood growing up out here, so he's like my brother."

"Okay! I think I might take Abbey up on her invitation and come out tomorrow for a visit!"

"Oh! Okay! Then, you will have to get a mud map from Eileen at the main house to tell you were to come.

Otherwise you could get very lost and that would be horrible."

"That's all right, Katrina, don't stress. I will see you tomorrow. Bye for now!"

"See ya!"

They arrived at the shed and unloaded the horses into their stalls, made sure they had water and unpacked the car. The two girls then helped with settling the other horses from the truck and taking all the food and camping supplies into the shed.

Once they were all set up, the group stopped for a quick lunch and a coffee. After lunch everyone saddled up their own horses and went to round up the first lot of cattle. They were going to round up the cattle that were in the first paddock, and closest to the yards. The other paddocks would take nearly the whole day to run around in.

Kat was on Molly, a chestnut mare about eight years old. It had been a while since she had ridden but it was like riding a bike, you never forgot what to do. She knew Molly and they had ridden together heaps of times, she was a safe quiet horse.

Abbey on the other hand was on a young grey gelding about three years old, just broken and just getting used to being worked with these horses and the cattle.

They cantered off down the paddock trail and when they reached the bottom fence line of the paddock, Abbey and Andy went to the far side and Jared and Kat stayed this side, they all spread out and then started to walk back towards the way they had come, picking up the cattle on the way.

Several hours later they all returned to the shed with the first delivery of mixed cattle. Some of the heifers were very pregnant and walking slowly. Other heifers had newly born calves running beside them, and some were so tiny they could have been only hours old. The rest were young steers and a few breeding bulls.

Once they were all locked up and safe in the yards, they took care of their own horses. A good hour later they had finished for the day, and it was their turn for a shower and dinner.

"So you think you are going to be able to walk tomorrow?" Jared asked passing Kat a cold beer.

"It's been a while but I'll be all right, can't let the side down, ah!"

"No, you can't and just because you are dating some royal shifter doesn't give you special treatment," said Andy.

"Did I ask for special treatment? No I did not! So back off! Hairy legs!" Kat said as everyone laughed.

The next day everyone got in and helped sort the cattle in the yards. After drenching them all, Abbey and Andy released all cows and their calves, the pregnant heifers and the breeding bulls to a large paddock that had been rested through the summer. Whilst Jared and Katrina mustered the separated steers back down the dirt road to one of the fattening pastures. They would stay there until they were sent off to market, and would also need to be nearer the main house yards as they were the ones that caused the most trouble.

They were walking the horses back to the cattle yards when they both heard a car coming along the road. Jared became very protective and moved closer to Kat, she turned to see a gold colour car and knew it was Zach coming. When he got nearer Jared and Kat stopped to let him get past, but he stopped and got out of the car.

"Hey, Zach, we won't be long if you want to go ahead, Abbey and the other guys are at the shed."

He started to walk towards the horses, when they started to fidget and prance. He stopped when Jared reached over to grab Molly's reins.

"Sorry, I seemed to have affected your horses."

"It's all right. We won't be long."

He got back in the car and drove off slowly to the shed.

"Wow! That was weird; normally shifters are okay with an animal. That makes me think he's something else."

"Jared, what do you think he is? A lion shifter. That would explain the horses playing up, lions eat horses right."

"No, I think he's something else, but he can't be! That would make him the rarest shifter in the world."

"Jared, you are starting to freak me out, should I be running? I cannot believe there are so many secrets with you lot."

"Don't worry, I will ask him! I am not letting you anywhere near him until we know!"

They arrived back at the shed and went and put the horses away in the stalls. Jared was very quiet until they reached the shed and found everyone sitting outside, drinking coffee and beer. Zach stood up and walked towards Kat, but Jared pulled her behind him. Zach stopped dead in his tracks and waited to see what was going on.

"Is everything all right, Katrina?"

"I am sorry but I don't feel happy about Kat coming anywhere near you until you let us know what sort of shifter you are?" Ignoring Jared, Zach carried on talking to Katrina.

"Katrina, I didn't know your family here were shifters, until I met Eileen at the house. My bloodline is Lion and Eagle if that answers your question. You must be Jared, is it?"

"Jared, that's enough!" said John. Jared's eyes had gone all black and he was protecting her, his arms held out, blocking her from going to Zach.

"No, Dad. I am sorry but it's not. Kat's human and this guy could be either lion or eagle or something else. He can manipulate her into doing anything he wants and she wouldn't have any idea what she was doing, until he had finished with her."

"That I have already worked out for myself," Kat said.

Zach's eyes were glowing a brighter gold now and Kat could tell he was getting very angry, this was getting pretty scary. He could shift at any time, to what, they didn't know.

"I would never hurt her; she is my life and chosen mate. I have never wanted anything so much in my life, like I want her. I am in love with her and need her to trust me for what I am and what I become."

"So I will ask you again, because I want to hear it from you. What sort of shifter are you?"

"A griffin."

"But that's not possible," said John. There was a gasp from Abbey and Andy.

"I knew it all the time, but I wanted to hear it from you," Jared said.

"It is true. Can I touch my mate now?"

"Yes, of course. I wanted to make sure you were worthy of her, because we love and care for her like she's our own."

"I can see that, and thank you for caring for her so much. It means a great deal to me."

Zach hugged and kissed Kat whilst everyone calmed down and then Zach walked over and shook Jared's hand.

"Well, I know where to come when I need a bodyguard to protect her."

"Do you really think it would come to that?" Jared asked.

"You are the only other people I have told, apart from my close family. Once it gets out what I am, I think it's going to attract a lot of shifters. Some good, others might have other ideas, I really don't know."

"How is that even possible, Zach? I mean you are half eagle like your mother and half lion like your dad. I thought griffins were something from Greek mythology."

"No, they are real, or they were back in central Asia and about a thousand years after the Bronze Age roughly 1950 BC.

"Well, we don't need to mention anything; it was only two nights ago that we told Kat about our little secret and she has been living with us off and on most of her childhood."

"Yeah. I hate secrets and lies. Can you tell me what a griffin is?" Kat asked.

"Can you take the rest of the afternoon off? I'd like to show you something. I will bring you back later."

"Yes, okay! But I need to have a shower and get out of these dirty clothes."

"Okay, I'll wait for you."

She ran to the shower and found some clean clothes on the way; she was determined to get back there before Jared could give Zach any more grief. When Kat came out fifteen minutes later there was no sign of Jared or Abbey and Andy. Only John and Zach and they had their heads together. They were talking in great detail when they looked up and saw her approaching.

"You all right if I take off for a while, John?"

"Sure. Take some lunch with you, none of you have eaten yet!"

She packed up some sandwiches, fruit and some water and threw them all in a bag. Zach opened the car door for her and she climbed in. They drove off, leaving the guys behind to finish the work for the afternoon.

They drove back to the Williams's property but instead of going up to the homestead like before, Zach took another lane to the right and followed a small driveway through trees and high bushes. Kat could see nothing through the bushes, it was very private wherever they were going. She watched him pull up and turn the car off.

"Come on, I have something to show you."

He took her hand and she followed him through the trees to a small clearing. There were some huge black boulders in front of them and a small creek running through the land. There were smaller boulders in the water and with the running current they became falls forming the cascading water. It was very soothing listening to the waterfalls. Kat looked up into Zach's eyes and smiled, "This is really lovely."

"I thought of you when I found it. That's not all, come on, there's more."

They walked along the creek for a while and there, hidden in the trees, was a small cabin. It was like the ones around his parents' home.

"Do you have a lot of these cabins hidden all over the property?"

"Yes there are a few around. I think the Harrises had them all built for the tourist season.

"How many are there altogether?"

"There are four up near the homestead and this one. But there could be more, we have not covered all the ground yet."

"Wouldn't it be easy to ask the real estate?"

"Yes, but it's fun finding them, come and have a look."

They walked towards the cabin and climbed up the little log steps to the veranda. Zach opened the front door for her and she poked her head around it, to see what was in there.

She found a small lounge with a wood burner in the corner of the room, next to it a large number of chopped logs. Red check curtains, hanging in the small timber windows and the same material made up in cushions on the lounge and a table cloth covering the table. It was lovely; there was a small kitchenette with a fridge and microwave to cook with. When she walked into the bedroom, she found a good-sized double bed with a timber cupboard and *en-suite* with a large shower and toilet.

"This is lovely, Zach, I feel like I am Goldilocks."

"Good I am glad you like it. I will go and get the food out of the car and we can have a picnic."

Kat hadn't realised how hungry she was until they started eating the sandwiches. Zach went to the fridge and brought out a bottle of champagne. She looked up, surprised, to see his face a picture of happiness. He could not stop grinning.

He passed her a glass of the bubbling wine and she drank it quickly. It was sweet and fruity and maybe a little strong. He came and sat with her on the couch and refilled her glass.

"Are you trying to get me drunk?" She thought it was giving her a little confidence.

"I don't need to; remember I can do this!"

He bent down and kissed her, his eyes were glowing bright and they held her fast. She could no longer look away from his eyes and was truly hypnotised by his presence. She felt as if his eyes were draining out everything in her brain. She could certainly see how snakes could mesmerise and kill their prey, moving away was not an option. Her arms circled his neck and pulled him nearer to her body; his tongue pushed her lips open and slid into her mouth. As he twisted his tongue around with hers it was sending signals to her brain and there was an instant rush of warmth and excitement spreading through her body. Kat's nipples stood up hard and there was a tightness growing in her stomach, going straight down to her thighs.

"I want to be with you, Zach."

"Kat, are you sure?" Smiling, to herself, she just realised what he called her.

"I love the way you call me Kat and I want you to make love to me."

Zach's eyes changed back to their normal hazel eyes. He looked at her and stroked the side of her face with his fingers.

"Are you sure now, that I am not using any power to control you?" Kat laughed and nodded.

He took her by the hand and they walked together into the bedroom. Her heart had started to race and so she took another large sip from the champagne. Kat put the glass down on the cupboard and turned around to face him.

"I have not been with anyone, in years."

"It's all right we can go as slowly as you like."

He took his time to undress her, firstly taking off her jumper and then the shirt. He then sat her down on the bed and pulled off her boots one at a time, followed by the socks and then her jeans until she was left sitting in just a bra and panties. Then he came and sat down beside her and pulled her hair loose from its ties, dropping it all in thick waves around her shoulders. He pulled the back of Kat's head towards him and slowly kissed her. Every nerve in Kat's body was waking up and he was suddenly taking too long.

Her hands went under his shirts and tugged them free from his jeans. She pushed his shirt and tee-shirt up higher and higher until they had to stop kissing for the clothes to go over his head. He had a god-like chest, covered in thick tight bulging muscles and an eight-pack that finished just below his jeans. Her hands glided over those muscles until she grabbed what she was seeking, the buttons to his flies. He stood up and pulled his boots off then his jeans and then lifted her up and laid her under the blankets. He crawled in beside her and they started to kiss again, this time a lot more heated. His tongue was running up and down her lips, and then making circles around her tongue. He wriggled out of her mouth, with his tongue and made his way across her neck, kissing and sucking as he went. Her hands were stroking his lower back up to his shoulders and back again. Kat could feel two small mounds on either side of his shoulder blades; she stopped and looked up at him.

"Will I get to see them?"

"Yes, my love, but not right now, I am busy."

He disappeared under the blankets and the next thing she felt was her bra clasps being released and her breast becoming free. His tongue reached one of her nipples and she gasped, the pleasure was too much. Nothing had ever felt this good; he was licking, sucking and squeezing them with his fingers. He stroked her rib cage and stomach with his free hand drawing circles as he moved towards her thighs. Then he peeled away Kat's panties.

Oh! My God, this is really happening, she thought.

"I was thinking coming home had never been so much fun," she said to him when his long fingers pushed in between her thighs and he inserted them into her wet entrance. Katrina grabbed his boxers and started to pull them down so she could feel his skin close to hers. His penis sprang out and was released instantly and she took hold of it in her fingers, rubbing it slowly up and down. She couldn't take his fingers any more, she was going to climax. Kat pulled the tip of his penis to her opening and hoping he'd get the message to pull his fingers away. He did, he came out from under the blankets and worked his way, kissing all back up her body and then when they had eye contact he thrust his huge length inside her welcoming entry. Kat let out a moan and he stopped whilst she stretched to accommodate his size. Then he started to move in and out, picking up speed until she reached her climax and called out his name. Her whole body shuddered, it was then Zach really started to move inside her, his eyes glowing a deep bronze, making her skin tingle and all the nerves pulsate through her body.

She reached another hard climax and he followed, shooting his seed deep within her.

He moved to her side and tucked Kat in to his chest, encircling her with his arms. They laid there for a while until they drifted off to sleep. It was much later he woke her with a kiss and suggested he took her back to the Hammonds' Farm.

He dropped Kat off after giving her a long kiss. She really wanted to go with him but she had a job to do here. He was really getting under her skin, what was she going to do next week when she headed back to Brisbane?

The six of them sat down to a late barbeque dinner that night and sorted out the jobs for the next day. Eileen had driven out with fresh salads and some homemade bread. John had decided they all go to the next large paddock as it would take them all to search for the cattle. This paddock was two kilometres wide and five kilometres in length with a large creek running up through the middle.

Every one welcomed a good cooked breakfast that morning from Eileen and it would see them through most of the day. When Kat went in to the horses, Molly was waiting for her but she noticed one of her shoes was missing and a nail was poking through her hoof. She called out to Abbey, who said she would have to take another horse until John could pull the nail out and re-shoe her. Kat hated that idea of a new horse but there was not much she could do about it. She kissed Molly on the nose and left to find the next mount. John told her to take Custer, a palomino gelding with a flaxen mane and tail. He was young but not as silly as the grey Abbey was riding. She threw the saddle cloth up over his withers and then placed the stock saddle on top, once she tied the girth and attached the saddle bag to the back of the saddle. They were carrying their own supplies of water and a little food. Kat pushed her new satellite phone in one of the pockets and strapped in the .22 magnum rifle Jared had given her.

They took off down the trail to the next mustering paddock and separated at the creek about half an hour down the track. Jared and Kat went straight along the fence line and Andy, Abbey and John went through the dry creek bed to the other side. They were to meet up later when the two groups had pushed the cattle back along the creek and the fence line.

Jared and Kat arrived at the boundary fence and turned around, she stopped and pulled out a bottle of water for a drink and offered some to Jared. He shook his head so she took several mouthfuls and put it away.

"So you two seem to be pretty serious, ah?"

"Well yes Jar, but I don't know, it's going to be hard when I get back to Brisbane. You know how long it took me to get this holiday, in between Rob's busy schedules. I don't know when I will get time off again to be away from the kids."

She picked up several head and drove them back towards Jared at the fence line.

"Don't worry, you will work it out!"

"I hope so."

"Look out! You've lost one."

Kat turned to see a small steer take off in the opposite direction, and cantered off to bring him back but he had other ideas. She followed him through the scrub and tried to push him back to the fence line.

He kept running into thicker scrub, taking her further away from where she had left Jared. Kat decided to pull up and turn around when she heard a loud hissing. Before she could register what had happened her horse started snorting and reared up in front of a taipan snake.

It was about 1.8 metres in length, brown in colour, with that unmistakable head. It sprang up to strike her horse twice in the chest and once on the leg. Custer reared up on his hind legs again to try and stamp on it, but when she screamed the gelding took off at a gallop and left her holding on for dear life. She tried several times to pull him up or turn him quickly but he was too freaked out.

Kat knew he had been bitten and that it was only a matter of time before the venom took hold. The venom is known to paralyse its victim's nervous system and clot the blood, which then blocks all the blood vessels, killing the animal.

The inland taipan is generally shy and not normally known for its aggressive nature as its cousin, the coastal taipan, but this snake was the mother of all evil. She could see her life flashing before her eyes, try as she may this horse was not going to stop.

After ten minutes of galloping they had arrived back at the creek where they were supposed to meet the guys in a few hours, with all the cattle they had rounded up.

Custer started to slow down and she thought it might be wise if she found somewhere to jump off.

He stumbled on the rocks and tripped. Kat could feel him going down so she raced to get her feet out of the stirrups to jump off. He fell on his side and she went down, with him. Kat screamed out in pain as her leg was crushed underneath him; she had landed between him and the sharp rocks. God, this couldn't be happening.

Custer's body was burning up above her leg and she could feel his heart hammering. She could see the poor horse's eyes rolling around in his head. If she could reach her gun, and could put him out of his misery, maybe that would help. Thinking about it there was no way she could do that. She was too close to the animal and might end up with the dead weight on her leg. She could also start a stampede if the other guys were near sending the cattle off in every direction. God this was the worst day of her holiday. She thought, *I need help; I must try and reach my phone in the saddle bag. Jared will know what to do.*

When she pulled herself up against the saddle her stomach twisted and the pain shooting down her left leg was incredible. She could see the pocket on the saddle bag that she had put the phone in, but it was too far to reach. *Why didn't he fall on his other side?* Kat thought.

The water was within reach so that was good! She could stay hydrated in the warm weather unless she was stuck there for a considerable length of time and no one found her. She wasn't going to risk it and started to yell for help.

She must have blacked out with the pain because the next thing she heard, someone was shouting her name. They were quite a distance away but that didn't stop her yelling out. She yelled back for what seemed hours, but could have been minutes and was so happy to see Jared and Zach running towards her voice. It was nearly dark, so she must have been there for a few hours.

"Oh! Shit! Kat, are you all right, what happened?" Jared said.

"What do you think? JARED! I was chasing that stupid freaking steer and the next thing we ran straight into a freaking taipan."

"Holy fuck, trust you to run into a taipan."

"Yes, very bloody funny Jar, that's not how I would put it. My phone is in the saddle bag but I could not reach it."

"It's all right, we will get you out Kat. We will just need to lift this dead horse off you first," Zach said.

"Oh! Is he dead? Poor fella, I was starting to like him, since Molly let me down."

"Kat, Jared and I are going to have to shift to pull this horse off you. Then when it's moved we will be able to see how bad your injuries are. We just need you to hold on until the pain relief arrives. Okay!"

There were some headlights coming along the dirt road and the noise of a four-wheel drive rumbling. It stopped in a hurry and more people got out. John raced across the creek with the first aid kit.

"Okay, Katrina honey, how are you feeling?"

"Like shit. You?"

"Still witty as ever, that's good Kat, but if you wanted the morning off you should have asked," said Abbey.

"We have some pain killers we are going to give you before the horse is lifted off you," said John.

"Thanks that would be good. I can't feel my toes."

John turned around and looked at Zach. They seemed to communicate without saying anything.

"How long have you been looking for me?"

"Honey, you been gone for nearly six hours," said John.

John rolled up Kat's sleeve and pulled out a needle full of something, she was not worried what was in the syringe, she just hated needles.

Zach seemed to feel her pain and said. "It's okay! It will help, numb the pain and then we can lift this horse off you."

71

"I don't like needles," and she curled her bottom lip up like a child who was going to cry. He laughed and kissed her.

"Come on, you have to be a brave warrior, it's only a little prick."

"I will need another kiss."

He signalled to John, then leant over and kissed her while John gave the injection.

Kat could feel the warm fluid running through her blood stream and found it was relaxing, and helping with all the pain she had felt.

Jared and Zach started to take off their coats someone cried out something about a helicopter landing and she started to drift.

"I want to see you change," she said as the walls caved in around her and she blacked out.

Chapter 5

Katrina woke up to find herself in a white room connected and surrounded by beeping machines. She started to move but was held fast by something heavy. She looked down to find Zach asleep on her mattress with one of his arm across her waist. The OBs machine attached for her blood pressure, temperature and oxygen levels started beeping faster. A nurse rushed into the room, to find her patient awake.

Hello, Katrina, I am so glad to see you have woken up. You've had us all worried. How are you feeling? Do you need any pain relief?"

"Where am I?" she asked looking around. The nurse continued to play with the monitors on the machines.

"You are in Townsville General Hospital, in the surgery ward. You have broken your leg in two places. I will ask the Doctor the come in and explain what he has done through the surgery to put your leg back together. You were very lucky someone found you in time. You had some internal bleeding too but the doctors have stopped that. I hear you had a fall on a horse?"

"Yes, he got bitten by a snake and then fell and collapsed on top of me."

"Well you are very lucky, dear, good job your fiancé and your brother found you."

The nurse smiled and kept looking at Kat and then to Zach, who was still fast asleep with his arm across her.

When she walked out of the door Zach put his head up. Bringing his arm back across Kat's body, he stopped to hold her face in his hand.

"God, I was so worried. Jared thought he saw which way you had taken off, but when he followed your tracks there was too much chinee apple scrub and thick undergrowth, he rode back for help. Once everyone was alerted they rang me, and I came straight away. Your satellite phone should have given us a GPS reading so we could track your position, but it didn't work. If Jared and I hadn't found you when we did I don't know what I would have done. I have only known you for a short time but you are the most important thing in my life. I am not letting you out of my sight ever again."

"I missed your shift. I wanted to see what a Griffin looked like. Not fair!"

"Kat, you blacked out from the pain and I don't think it would have been much fun spending all that time trapped underneath that horse. I promise to show you as soon as we get you out of here and we are back where I can look after you."

"How long have I been in here?"

"Well the accident happened on Thursday, we flew you straight here to Townsville and today is Saturday."

"What! It's Saturday already, I go back to work in a week!"

"That's not going to happen; you are going to be here for at least another four weeks."

"Hey! What do you mean you flew me straight here?"

"We have our own helicopter and Aaron is a very good pilot, actually we are all good at flying. He came to rescue you when I called him, and found Abbey. Abbey happens to be his mate. I can't believe we have both found our true mates."

"What! O.M.G I don't believe this! I miss all the good shit."

There was a tap at the door and her dad poked his head around the door.

"Can we come in?" They hugged and kissed their daughter.

"Hi! Mum and Dad, who's looking after the hotel?"

"We asked Hailey to stay in the hotel until we got back. She's has her husband with her, luckily he's home from the mine this week. Although Richard very kindly offered, to help us out."

They had been worried sick and after a while calmed down. Zach was helping, reassuring them that she would be well looked after and that he wasn't going to leave her side. They stayed about ten minutes and then said they would let the next two come in, and they would come back tomorrow for another visit.

Before anyone else came in the doctor walked in, with the nurse she had been talking to. After introductions Doctor Cameron checked all of Katrina's charts, her breathing and asked how she was feeling. He went into detail, explaining what procedure he had used during the surgery to pin the left tibia in two places. He explained that she had bruising to her kidneys from the fall onto the sharp rocks and some internal bleeding was due to broken ribs, puncturing her lung. He also told her that because she had a rare blood group they needed to fly blood down from Cairns urgently which prolonged her surgery and her recovery. It was decided that with total rest, she would be safe to leave in six weeks.

Zach thanked the doctor for his work in surgery and shook his hand. Kat also thanked him but was feeling miserable and getting depressed to find she was going to be stuck in hospital for six weeks. She was also wondering why she'd never been told about her rare blood group. Didn't people wear identity bracelets or necklaces for these sorts of emergencies? Why hadn't her parents told her? Zach walked over and touched her face with his hand.

"It's all right, we will get through this," Zach said.

"I never knew about my blood group, its funny Mum and Dad never mentioned it."

"You will have to ask them when they come back tomorrow."

"That's a long time being stuck in here, I will go mental! I hate hospitals."

"I think if all goes well, we might be able to work on that nice doctor to letting you go after a few weeks."

"How are you going to do that, Zach?"

"Honey don't worry about anything now; all you need to worry about is getting better."

Jared and Abbey knocked and rushed in, after two days Jared was still pale and freaking out.

"Oh! Thank God, Kat," Jared said as he hugged Katrina.

"He's been blaming himself for telling you to go chase that stupid cow," said Abbey.

"Come on Jar, how many years have we been mustering together? Not once have I seen a taipan out there, it was just bad luck."

"Now that you are awake and in good hands, we are going to head back to the station. We left Dad and Andy out there and they are snowed under with the rest of the mustering."

"Abbey, Zach tells me you and Aaron are a thing. How did that happen? You have to have some serious girl talk with me later. I want to know all the details, but not when this lot are around."

Abbey laughed and gave Katrina another hug and promised to fill her in on all the details over the next couple of days. After more hugs and reassurances they also left to head home. They had been told by John to wait there until Kat had woken up and make sure she was comfortable before leaving, which they would have done without hesitation.

Kat was starting to feel sleepy when Zach's brother Aaron came in a little later.

"I just rang Mum and Dad and let them know you were awake. They send their love and ask if you need anything, to let me know."

"I will be staying around with Zach until we can get you out of here and back to the Ridge," Aaron said.

"What about my job? I still need to work. I don't want to let Rob down and I really love those children, and my job. Couldn't I go back until they find a replacement for me?"

Tears were welling up in her eyes until they broke the sides and slipped down her cheeks. Zach wiped away the tears and looked at Aaron.

"We can talk about this later; you have only just woken up!" Zach whispered.

"Okay!" she said as she drifted off to sleep.

The next day the nurses removed her OBs machine and the IV; as she was now drinking fluids there was no need to keep them going.

Zach and Aaron had gone back to the hotel later that evening and managed to get some rest, at last relieved that Katrina was awake and on the mend.

They both looked refreshed when they came in the next day, and no dark shadows under their eyes. Zach brought in a bouquet of yellow daffodils that were in season and one red rose, he was such a romantic guy, Kat thought to herself. He was definitely a keeper.

The next two weeks flew by Katrina spending a lot of time sleeping and resting with all the medication the doctors had given her. She had spoken to Rob and the children several times and Rob had decided to cancel any tours he had to stay at home with the children. His mother had also decided to fly in from Perth and stay with them until Katrina's return so that was something she didn't need to worry about. She had also had plenty of phone calls from her parents and Abbey on her new satellite phone. She never did find out what happened to the old one.

Zach had not mentioned anything about Kat going back to work, but she could see he did not like the idea. She really needed to keep her independence as long as she could.

Her daily ritual of bed baths stopped after the end of the third week. She was then mobile with crutches and able to take a real shower with the help of a nurse, once her leg had been wrapped up to keep from getting wet. It was the first time she had been able to get her hair washed in weeks and it had been driving her nuts, being greasy and itchy. She felt more human being able to shower and happy now things were moving along. Kat could certainly see a light at the end of the tunnel.

On Friday morning of the fourth week, Katrina was going to be discharged from the hospital into the care of the Williams brothers. Doctor Cameron had somehow changed his mind about keeping Katrina in hospital for another two weeks. He had given them strict instructions on how to treat the leg and keep it dry. Doctor Cameron had also made it clear again, that if there were any problems at all to come back to the hospital. Zach and Aaron thanked the doctor and then discussed the best way of looking after Katrina.

"Pardon me, for butting in. But I am right here! I am a grown woman and can decide what's best for me!"

They both stopped talking and looked at her, suddenly both amused. She couldn't help smiling, looking at these two incredibly sexy guys, both very similar in looks.

"Firstly, I don't look anything like Aaron."

"You cheat, you were not supposed to read my mind," said Kat, going red.

"No! I am better looking than Zach, Kat," Aaron said laughing.

"Well, we were suggesting that if you need to keep the cast on for another three weeks, it would be better if you came to our place rather than your parents' place. All the bedrooms are upstairs and there's no way you are going to climb with that on."

"Oh! Okay, that makes sense" Looking down at the cast that ran from her foot and ankle up to the top of her knee. "What are my parents going to say?"

"I think you will find that your parents are very happy that Zach came up with the idea, because they are still flat out at the hotel with the tourist season," said Aaron.

"You make me sound like an inconvenience," said Katrina.

"Don't be silly. It's my job to take care of you and I want to take care of you and we are better equipped, that's all," said Zach. After the doctor had signed all her discharge papers and given her one last check over, all they needed to do was collect her medication and then they were at last on their way home. Everyone was happy to be leaving the hospital. Aaron could catch up with Abbey at last and head to Brisbane. Zach could have Katrina to himself without the nurses coming in all the time and Katrina could catch up with her families. They took the lift up to the roof where the helicopter was still parked, with Katrina in a wheelchair and their luggage. Aaron had been up earlier and taken all the covers off the blades so with a quick radio check and some clearance from the airport, they would soon be on their way back to Thistle Ridge. Zach lifted Katrina into the helicopter and laid her across the back seats and then strapped her in as best he could. He jumped in next to Aaron and five minutes later they were on their way.

They arrived back at the Ridge by lunch time and landed not far away from the main homestead and buildings. A couple of their workers ran over after the blades stopped, to help take some luggage inside the house. Zach picked Katrina up from the back seat and carried her in to the lounge. Once inside he put her into a recliner and wheeled it into the dining room where everyone was busy talking and where all the action was. Zach's parents embraced Katrina with hugs and Amy fussed around her making sure she was comfortable before lunch. Richard talked about the flight back and the Doctors report to Zach whilst passing around some drinks.

It seemed such a long time ago, when she had last visited their home on that Sunday. Remembering the lovely romantic ride she had taken with Zach on the quad bike and the coffee Zach had surprised her with.

Amy had prepared a large roast lunch to celebrate the family all being back together.

"We have invited your parents out on Sunday for lunch and to visit you, they are going to leave the cook in charge for a few hours, so they can both come," said Richard

"I wish my family didn't need to be kept in the dark. I don't think they are the sort of people to panic easily."

"It's all a little too soon; Katrina you didn't know there were shifters on this earth until a month ago. Give it some time, besides there is a lot you need to learn first about our history.

Please don't you worry it will be all right," Richard said.

"Well that will give you something to do, can't have my little sister getting bored now. Ah!"

"You know your just as funny as Jared; Aaron you two will get on well," said Kat

Katrina said no more and enjoyed her lunch with her newly acquired family. Later she excused herself to go and lay down, feeling tied from the journey and the medication the doctors had prescribed her. Zach picked her up and carried her to his rooms and laid her down on the bed. She still needed plenty of rest, and dragging this heavy leg around was not helping.

Zach came and laid down beside her, it was the first time they had been alone in weeks.

Kat moved so she was lying with her head on his shoulder and cuddled up to him and that's where she woke up several hours later. Zach had fallen asleep as well, and only stirred when she moved her hand up to his face. He kissed her hand and then bent down to kiss her on the lips. The kiss was gentle and soft; Zach was in no rush, moving his hands up and down her ribs and waist. Kat moved her fingers up underneath Zach's jumper and tee shirt to get to his soft skin. He pulled back to look at her.

"What are you doing Kat?"

"I want to play; it's been too long! And I want to see you naked."

He looked shaken and very amused at the same time.

"Yes, it has, but you are still injured with broken bones and the doctor said we had to take good care of you and let you rest for at least another week."

He was grinning now at her, his whole face radiating happiness. She loved it when he really smiled, he always looked so serious.

"You know, you should smile and laugh more often. It's good to see you relaxed."

"How about I let you be the doctor and I will be the patient?"

Zach burst out laughing and started to undress her.

"We are going to take this very carefully, and if I see any pain at all in your face or in your thoughts then we stop. Okay?"

Kat nodded her head while watching him take get care of removing her one=legged pair of jeans.

"Skirts would have made this easier if you had let us buy you some?"

"I know, but I don't like them and actually have never owned one. My uniform for work is smart long pants or trousers, you fellas might say."

Smiling at her, he finished all the undressing and laid her under the sheets and doona to keep her warm. Zach climbed in to bed with just his boxes on and curled up beside her. They kissed again and this time it was more heated, Zach kissed her with his tongue sending tingling messages down through her body and straight to her thighs. She stroked his back and shoulders making

82

circles around his wing slits. He kissed her neck and then moved down to her breasts, gently squeezing one with his fingertips whilst sucking her other nipple in his mouth. The sensation was sending her heart pulsating and he stopped to look up into her eyes.

His eyes were glowing bronze into her bright green eyes; he was reading her mind to make sure she was all right.

"Zach I'm fine please don't stop; I really want us to do this."

Zach reached up and kissed her on the lips, not using any body weight to learn on her and then went back to where he was.

He traced his fingers alone her left breast and down along her ribs down through her flat tummy to just above her thighs. It was so light it could have been a butterfly landing and then he did it again and again. She was getting so aroused that when he slipped his fingers down between her thighs he was met with her wetness. He looked up again to find her eye contact before pushing further into her welcoming folds.

She gasped out with pleasure as Zach slid his long fingers in and out of her vulva and then when she thought she could not take any more he bent down and with his mouth sucked her clitoris hard, making her climax. She covered her mouth, realizing she was going to scream out and his parents were still somewhere in the building.

Zach raised himself up and inserted his length into her wet entry. He was so gentle she didn't know how he was keeping himself so calm. His smouldering eyes kept her mesmerised and almost hypnotised as he started to move inside her. He kept a steady pace, trying not to jar her ribs with the pushing in and out until he reached a climax and came inside her. He joined her back on the mattress and wrapped his arms around her. Kissing the top of her head he said.

"Well that was easy? Not."

They both laughed and that was when Katrina held her ribs.

"Don't make me laugh, that's when my ribs hurt."

"Sorry Kat, I thought what we've just done might have hurt more."

"No that was great, you were very gentle you can do that to me any time," she said smiling.

"How about a warm shower, before dinner or do you want to sleep some more?"

"No more sleep, thanks or I will be awake all night."

"Well we don't want you awake all night so let's hit the shower, ah!" he said smiling.

"Whatever you say, doctor!"

Katrina and Zach joined the others for dinner and caught up with all the news of the farm while Zach and Aaron had been away.

"How are you going along with the hay, Craig?" Richard asked

"The hay is nearly ready for harvesting, we cut the last of the last twenty acres today. Ben was turning most of the day, with that new tractor. Clarke has been doing some maintenance on the baling machine. We think with another couple of days' turning the hay, we should be able to bale most of the hundred acres next week."

"Excellent work," Richard said.

"After that we would like to start bringing in the ewes to the big barn, just in case some of them wanted to lamb early."

"That's a good idea," Amy said.

Amy told them that other pack members were working in the gardens, at this time of the year they had potatoes to dig up. There were also pumpkins, spinach, lettuce and zucchini needing to be checked and picked every day. They had not been on the property very long but most keen gardeners were aware that the possums and bandicoots came in at night and helped themselves.

They were planning to put more vegetables in this year as the pack was getting larger and they all needed to eat. They were also going to supply the supermarket with fresh produce, earning them some income. The pack under Richard's rule tried to make the farm as self-sufficient as possible. He had decided to increase their stocks of cattle, bring in some sheep and goats from what the previous owner had kept. They were also going to build some bigger chicken pens so they could increase the numbers from fifteen up to forty laying hens.

"Wow, your plans are really taking shape, Dad," said Zach.

"How are you coming along with the tourist's idea?"

"I have been working on that while we have been away. Katrina gave me a few ideas as well."

"I did?"

"Yes, I did what you said and rang the real estate. They told me that there were at least another two larger cabins along that same creek bank. Mr Harris was a little foggy as to where they were and hadn't been down to that creek since his wife died, which was several years ago. You see, she used to look after all of the cabins and let them out to the tourists. He spent his time doing other things and left her to do everything."

"Well that's interesting and sad," said Kat.

"I think we can market the tourist centres for next year that will give us plenty of time to get the cabins ready, and build a walking track. We can advertise the log cabins, with or without catering. We can bring food down from the main house or we could build an open kitchen down near the cabins with barbeques, and maybe a pizza oven.

"We could organise camp fires and music, and I thought we could use the black boulders in the creek as a name. I am still working on the design for the web site but I have this so far and it needs tidying up.

"Black Boulders Retreat; Want to escape from the rat race, come and enjoy your vacation in our comfortable and warm log cabins. In a secluded natural woodland with clean and tidy walking tracks up through the mountain ranges. We can cater for all your own needs, or just self-catering available. All year round fresh water running creeks, to swim in and for a little fossicking. Maybe helicopter rides by appointment only?"

"That's great work, Zach and that will be another income we can build on," Richard said.

"Yes, that really is exciting, we could make homemade bread and biscuits and all sorts of things for them," said his mother.

"We will need to sort out rates for the accommodation and everything else like food or sightseeing. Tomorrow I'll go down with Kat and have a look at the cabins, once we locate them. Then we will report back to you with what needs to be done," said Zach

"You could introduce horse rides as well," Kat said.

"That would be entirely up to you, Katrina, if you want to take that on?" said Richard

"That's a good idea as long as I don't need to go near them," Zach said.

"Yes, what is that all about? You seemed to spoke our horses when you called in to see me at the Hammonds' the other week."

"I am not sure. They just don't like me and they dance around being stupid."

"It was more like they thought they were going to get eaten."

The whole family started to laugh, looking at poor Zach.

"Well on that note I think it's time to turn in."

Katrina thanked Amy and Richard for the lovely dinner and was carried back to their rooms. Zach sat her down on the lounge chair in front of the fire.

"I am sorry if I said anything wrong!"

"It's all right. I just don't know why they do that, the horses I mean. It's always been that way, that's why we have never had any horses where we have lived."

"Maybe it's your scent or something. I mean, you are in human form when they see you? What about your father? Does he have the same problem?"

"Yes, but he seems to calm them or something. He's never ridden them though."

"Well maybe you don't use horses, we can think of something else. What about mountain bikes or camels?" she said, laughing.

"No, it's a really good idea using the horses, you could do trail rides up the mountain side once we cut a good path. Or you could do rides on the flat ground around the planted crops and ending up at one of the creeks for a swim. Because there will be you and Abbey both joining the family and you could run the stables and to do the rides."

"Wow! What about my job?"

"Well, I am hoping that you will marry me and stay here."

"Did you just propose?" Kat asked.

"Not yet, I haven't bought you a ring, silly!"

"Oh!"

"I am designing one to be made, but first I need to show you something. Because you may not want to marry me, and instead run off screaming to your parents."

Zach took Kat by the hand and pulled her off the couch. He picked her up and a throw rug that was on the back of the lounge and carried her to the garden. Zach embraced her with the warm rug and helped her to a chair. He took several deep breaths before asking her if she was ready.

"Yes," she said and nodded.

Katrina looked straight into his eyes and smiled, Zach started to shimmer and the light around him was as bright as it had been when Abbey and her family transformed.

She never took her eyes off him and when he finished shifting, she just gasped. Standing in front of her was the most beautiful creature she had ever seen. His eyes still hypnotised her but the body was different. Instead of a man standing in front of her there stood a huge eagle with a lion's body and tail. His head was now covered with light brown and golden feathers, pointed ears and a sharp hooked beak that could do a lot of damage. The feathers in darker shades now, went down through his beautiful chest and blended in to his front bird legs and down to his huge black talons. The feathers then extended along to his shoulders or where his shoulders would be, to a pair of massive wings. The wing feathers were a darker brown, with black and gold running through them. From there the feathers disappeared and were replaced with fur in a light tan and white. Following down the back legs and there she could see the lion's feet. His tail was similar in the tan colour, but instead of having a lion's tail with hair on the end it looked more like a weapon, she thought.

"You are the most beautiful thing I have ever seen. Can I touch you?"

Zach walked nearer to her and he dropped his huge head towards her lap. She stroked the feathers on his head and face they were so soft. Feeling a little more relaxed, she asked if she could touch his wings. He walked past her and pulled one open for her to view and then turned his head to see what she was thinking.

"Can you carry someone on your back?"

"Yes, but I never have," he said but not to her, she heard it in her head.

"Did you just say yes in my head? Holy crap, how did you do that?"

"I told you we would be able to do things a little differently after I claimed you."

"Oh! I thought you meant you were going to bite me, like werewolves do in books." They both laughed.

"No. Were-wolves, bears and lions do. Maybe vamps and pumas do, but I am not a hundred percent sure. We do it differently; the griffin marks you as his own, when he penetrates you naturally with his seed and you will also pick up my scent. You probably won't notice the difference as you are human but to a shifter it will be very noticeable. (My scent that is.) Other shifters will know that you belong to me and if they are smart enough they won't come near you. If anyone should ever come near you in a hostile way, I will kill them. No questions asked!"

"Wow, just like that?"

"Yes. I told you, you are my life and there's nothing more important than you! I will always be there to protect you and if I can't be there then my brothers will."

"Those poor guys, don't they have their own lives to be getting on with?"

"Not if I need them, which comes first. I am the first born so they will always be my guards."

"Hang on a minute. If you are real, then werewolves are too."

"Yes of course, but there are no other packs in this area. The werewolf is mostly found over in America and Canada. The same as goes for bears and pumas, those shifters try and stick around their animals' own habitat. Therefore, if they are seen by humans by mistake someone would think it was real animal and not a shifter."

"I have so much to learn."

Zach walked over and put his massive head on her shoulder. She naturally started to stroke him like you would a cat or a dog. He released a humming noise into her ear. It was very soothing almost like a cat purring. He started to shimmer and return back into his own body with his head still on her shoulder he said, "Thank you for not running away from me, I love you so much!"

"I can't run away now. I am falling in love with you."

Zach could not believe his ears, he was so happy, he had wanted her to love him and his griffin too. He picked Kat up and kissed her gently on the mouth and then carried her back inside. Later that evening they made love again, but this time in the most gentle way,

Zach taking his time, loving every part of her body and she too enjoying his body. There was no longer the need to rush any more, as they were now committed to each other with all body and soul.

Chapter 6

The next morning, showered and dressed, they planned their attack on the cabins. Katrina, with the help of Jenny, one of the wives from the pack, sorted out some lunch and drinks for them while Zach packed up some cleaning gear, tools and a heavy chainsaw.

He loaded up the truck with all their gear first before coming in and picking up Kat. Once they were down there she was hoping that she might be able to hobble around with her crutches. They passed the first cabin that had been their own hideaway and continued further down the lane. They kept driving for another five minutes when Kat spotted something between the trees.

"Hey Zach, pull up a minute. I think I see something."

"Good girl, I was beginning to think we might need the helicopter to help us find them."

He reversed the truck to where Kat had seen something and stopped. He got out and went for a closer look. "There's one over there, the undergrowth has grown up so I am going to need to cut us a path."

"Sorry I can't help you, maybe next month when they take this cast off. Your father has given me some reading material on your history, so I can read about you while I wait."

"Sounds good." Zach started up the chainsaw and walked off to the tree line. It was several hours later when he returned to collect her and she was halfway through one of books.

"Having fun?" he asked, all sweaty.

"This book is very interesting; I am learning so much." He laughed and went to grab a cold bottle of water out of the esky. He brought one back for her and put it in her lap.

"Are you ready to check out this cabin? It looks a lot bigger from the outside."

"Does a shifter's eyes glow in the dark?" He opened the truck door and leaned in and kissed her passionately on the lips before picking her up. She swung her arms around his neck and learned in close to his chest.

"I could get used to all this lovely treatment. You really are a caring man, I might just keep you," she said, kissing his cheek. Zach turned and looked at her, his eyes shining bright with amusement.

"I'll keep you to that, my damsel in distress. Now let's see what this cabin has to offer us, and then I'll walk back and get our lunch."

When they arrived at the log cabin it too was cosy and inviting from the outside. There was a small veranda like the other one and some old wicker chairs that had seen better days. When they went inside they found all the furniture still intact but very dusty. There was a strong closed-up, musty smell through the whole place. Kat hobbled over to a window and opened it, to let some fresh air in.

It had the same design log burner in the lounge fire place, for heating and hot water. As they walked down the hall way from the lounge they found two large bedrooms which included queen beds, bedside cupboards and small built-in wardrobes. At the end of the hall they found a bathroom, a toilet, and another small room that was empty. Coming back through the lounge they noticed the kitchen was also larger, with more benches and cupboards housing a standalone fridge freezer; a gas stove, a microwave, and a dining room table with four chairs.

"This one could be self-catering as it has a decent gas stove and the larger kitchen. We will need an electrician to check out all the electrical wiring and all the white goods first, as we might be up to replace all of these items. They never do any good being turned off for a long time."

"It's such a shame, to see these cabins run down. I bet Mrs Harris would be devastated," Kat said.

"The small bedroom could be an office, not that guests would want to be working. Or maybe we can add some bunk beds for children," Zach said.

"That's a better idea, families do have children!"

"I think we will need to throw out all the bedding, there is too much mould in the linen and curtains. I don't think any detergent is going to clean them up. Hopefully the mattresses on the beds will be okay if they're taken outside and aired for a few days," Kat said.

"First we will have some lunch and then I'll see about getting some help. You still need to rest that leg, remember!"

"I can't sit down all day, it's driving me mad."

Zach came back with some lunch and her crutches, although she seemed to be hobbling all right without them. Kat had already started to strip the linen off one of the beds and pulled the curtains down when he called out.

"I rang and spoke to Dad, he is sending down Terry, our head maintenance man and a couple of the wives from the pack.

"He also told Aaron to come down as he is moping around."

"Poor Aaron needs to catch up with Abbey. Can't he go down to Brisbane and visit her?"

"No, not yet, he's needed here."

They sat down for lunch and the conversation stopped as people started to arrive. Zach went off to meet them and tell them what he needed help with. The two wives, Anna and Carole, walked up and introduced themselves to Katrina and shook her hand. They were at the barbeque lunch she came to a few weeks ago but they were busy working in the kitchen.

They left Kat to finish her lunch and went inside to start cleaning the cabin. Terry and Zach made a list of items that needed updating, replacing or was just broken and what materials they need to buy for each job. While Aaron went off on his own, to find the other log cabin, with the aid of another chainsaw.

Before the end of the day, the cabin had been spring cleaned, all the furniture polished and all the bedding, curtains and cushions removed, to be discarded. The outside had been swept and the windows cleaned. Tomorrow they would work on the garden. They thought that by the end of the week, they would have the gardens back as they once were, although they would still need to replace some plants, where there were gaps. But there was no rush, they could be added later.

Aaron had found the other cabin further down the lane and it too was in need of some major cleaning. He was excited to find a small well next to the cabin when he started to clear the shrubbery.

"These cabins are amazing, I think they will make great holiday destinations for tourists trying to get away from the city life for a few days or weeks and when they are not in use, maybe we can use them?"

"I was already thinking about moving us into the first cabin, while we're working down here. Then I can carry on through the evenings tinkering with odd jobs. We can stop at the cabin on the way, to see what supplies we'll need to stay down here and I will light the wood burner," said Zach.

"I like your way of thinking; I have plenty of things that could be tinkered with."

They both burst out laughing.

After collecting some clothes, food and a small barbeque they made their way back to their little cabin. Katrina loved its cosiness and finally being on their own. They could discuss anything down here away from the family, without the worry of being overheard. Shifters had excellent hearing and nothing around the family was private.

Katrina unpacked the groceries and put them away in the kitchen.

"We've got steak tonight, a nice T-bone. I can do a green salad and stick some jacket potatoes in the microwave?" Kat said.

"Sounds good. I'll go outside and set the barbeque up and check how the fire's going."

Katrina laughed to herself; this was the best fun she'd had in ages. Just the two of them, hanging out, doing normal things together. This was how she could really get to know him, and find out everything else that was going on.

They sat outside talking about the cabins and what they could do with them making notes as they ate their dinner. Once the temperature dropped they moved inside and curled up in front of the log fire.

Zach excused himself for a minute to go to felt something. He came back with a little box in his hand.

"I have a little present for you!"

Zach passed Katrina a little blue jewellery box and her heart started to beat too fast.

"It's not what you are thinking it is. So just open it, you chicken."

She laughed and opened the box. Inside was a lovely necklace made in heavy gold with burnt yellow stones and diamonds in a flower design.

"It's beautiful, are those yellow sapphires? Zach, I can't accept this, it's too much."

"Yes, they are. And it's only the start, Katrina. Being my mate, you will need to get used to this. I will be giving you all sorts of treasures."

"Okay. Well, thank you, it's lovely. It's only I have never been in a relationship where someone took such care of me."

"I need to tell you something and I would really appreciate you keeping this close to your chest. Meaning I don't want this discussed with anyone else, not even your parents.

"Griffins have a fetish for gold, hence the gold car, all gold furnishings and just everything gold. This is because griffins are very similar to dragons, they both love gold and all sorts of valuable treasures. Both shifters like collecting gold items and they either buy or steal to keep their habits going. Dragons have also killed to get the things they want but we don't need to go that far, as we can use hypnosis."

"Oh!"

"Katrina, we have gold here in these small creeks and river beds and Mr Harris didn't realise it, being human. But this place has a lot of gold here. I was able to feel it when we first arrived, with the real estate agent. I can even smell it, especially down here near the water.

Dad and I have been looking for something like this for years. We did not want to attach the wrong sort of shifters to our pack, and that's why most of our group are either hawks or wild cats as they don't have the same fetishes. Tourism and growing vegetables and stock is only a cover up for what we are really doing."

"So please accept this with my love, and anything else I give you as a token of my deepest admiration for you."

"Thank you, Zach. I love it. Did you find the sapphires here as well?"

"No, they were found at a place called Tomahawk Creek, not too far from here."

"Can you show me how to pan for gold?"

"Yes, when your leg is better. You need to be standing in the creek or on the side and your leg will certainly get wet if we try now."

"Is that why Aaron's still here?"

"Yes."

"What aren't you telling me?"

Just as he opened his mouth to answer the question, the phone rang. Zach answered it and walked away from Katrina a little. He stood there for a while listening to the other person on the phone. Katrina decided she would leave them to it, and go and have a shower before bed. She was strapping her leg up when Zach came into the bedroom.

"That was Dad, his physic abilities are sending out a warning that there is something bad on the horizon. He's not sure where it's coming from, but the air is not right and it either means trouble is coming or it will be somewhere close by! He's getting all the pack together tonight for a meeting. They have all been told to be on the look out for anything suspicious."

"Will it seem strange if you are not there?"

"No, he will let them know that we are missing from the meetings as we are bonding, or humans like to call it honeymooning!"

"Well, don't tell my parents, because they will be expecting a human wedding in a church before that! You will need to make me your legal wife, in their eyes."

"Humans are funny, don't you think? They want a piece of paper to bind their marriage, where shifters, if lucky, find their true mate, bind with blood during claiming or their partner's seed."

"Don't you think that there is always going to be a problem with opening the place to tourists? They are all strangers, after all."

"Without being disrespectful to you, humans are not a threat. We will be able to sense straight away if another shifter encroaches on our territory. They normally have to ask for permission to be in another territory belonging to another pack.

"Dad also said that he's decided to have a pack meeting everyday now, instead of once a week, so he can keep tabs on all the members and find out if anyone has any problems. The rest of the flock members in town will be able to communicate by phone."

"How many pack or flock members do you have?"

"Only about fifty here, we like to keep small and that way, we stay discreet."

"Wow, that's still a lot of people, are they living all around here?"

"Yes. But you don't want to know about all that now. What were you doing?"

Katrina looked at him and smiled, without speaking she told him.

"I was just about to go in the shower, did you want to come in and wash my back?"

"Oh! Yes please," he answered her.

Zach helped Katrina take the rest of her clothes off and then carried her to the bathroom. He quickly lost all his clothes and joined her in the shower. The hot water was refreshing after a long day. Zach took some soap from the dispenser and started to wash her back, using his hands to massage her shoulders and neck. She was in heaven, it was so relaxing, his hands so gentle and strong at the same time working into her muscles.

She tried to turn around to do his back, but he hadn't finished. Instead he grabbed some more soap from the dispenser and worked all the way down her back through to her thighs and buttocks with his soapy hands.

"My turn," she said, grabbing the soap and making him turn around. He laughed and then she worked the soap into his neck muscles and all the way down to his waist. She reached his buttocks and stretched her hands around the front of him to his loins. He turned slowly and let her massage his manly length which by now was standing to attention. She worked it backwards and forwards with the soap until he took her hand away. He in turn grabbed some more soap and pushed his fingers between her thighs. She was so ready for him, he stopped and picked her up and grabbing her bottom, lined up his penis into her wet entry. He started to move slowly at first until he was comfortable with his footings, and she was securely holding on to him, then his body gained momentum, increasing in speed until they were both calling out with their own climaxes.

After their climaxes calmed down and their breathing steadied, they finished their shower and crawled into bed.

The light of the afternoon sun woke them and looking at his clock, Zach was shocked to see it was already twelve thirty.

"Holy crap, look at the freaking time!"

"Morning, or is it already afternoon, I know I'm starving," Kat said.

"Well that's got to be the most sleep we had since the hospital and returning home."

"I'll say. Let's see what we can find for brunch!" Kat said, grabbing a bath robe and hobbling up.

"That's a good idea; I will get dressed and find some timber to stoke up the wood burner. Then maybe we can start gardening at the cabin."

They spent the rest of the day in the other cabin's garden, Zach trimming all the bushes and digging up the soil to make new flower beds, while Katrina made a list of all linen, towels, bedding and furniture that they would need to furnish this cabin. She also checked the kitchen cupboards to see what was there, in the way of cooking equipment and utensils. Finding it a little sparse, she decided to start from scratch and order everything new from saucepans, to crockery and cutlery.

They finished later that evening and, forgetting that her parents were coming to tea, made a mad rush up there to see them. Luckily they hadn't arrived when the two of them pulled up in the truck near the house. Zach quickly shot into the shower while Katrina strapped her leg up with a bag.

They were still getting dressed when Katrina's parents arrived.

"Oh, this is bad. I should be out there."

"I'll run out and meet them and introduce them to everyone," said Zach

They needn't have worried because Richard had them all laughing. Zach came back into the bedroom.

"Dad's got it all sorted."

Zach picked up and carried Katrina out and sat her in one of the lounge chairs. Both her parents rushed over to hug her.

"Sorry, Mum and Dad, we got carried away down at the boulders with cleaning the cabins and didn't realise what the time was."

"I thought you were supposed to be resting for at least another three weeks. What's this cleaning about?" said her father.

"I was resting. When I mean cleaning, Zach was doing all the work. I was just keeping him company and doing a stock take."

"Sounds interesting, what are you guys up to?" asked Charlie.

Zach and Richard filled Charlie and Mary in about the boulders. Explaining what they were hoping to do with the cabins for tourism, whilst they sat down and ate dinner.

Charlie thought it was an excellent idea, bringing more wealth to the tiny town. He would also be able to send overflows from the pub out to them as well.

"I like the idea of getting my daughter back here. I have always hated the idea of her going to Brisbane. We could certainly use her skills at the hotel now and then."

"Yes, that would be lovely. I miss having her around," said Mary

All in all, it was a good evening. Amy and Mary chatted away on their own interests, catering and their different ideas for function parties and recipes.

At the end of the evening they all arranged to get together again and all went their separate ways. Zach carried Katrina to the truck and took her back to the cabin. He walked back into the warm and cosy cabin and sat her down in front of the wood burner.

"Well I am glad that went okay! I was worried."

"Why were you worried?"

"I don't know, your Dad had already met my parents. I suppose I just wanted everything to work out. My mother was at college with your dad! Did he say anything to you?"

"No, he didn't."

"Well, after she met him the other day, Mum really went quiet for a while, it was strange."

"If they have a past, I am not going to bring that up, maybe we just let it slide."

"Yes, that's a good idea, we won't mention it again," said Kat.

Zach opened a bottle of wine and poured out two glasses. They sat enjoying the warmth from the fire until they started yawning and decided to go to bed.

After breakfast, they started discussing the cabins.

"There's a lot of things to buy to get these cabins up and running. I have finished the list for the second cabin, and I am thinking we are probably going to need the same for cabin three. I have not checked this one yet, although it seems to be pretty good."

"Yes, that's a good idea. We could go and check the other cabin out this morning"

"We are going to have to make up names for these cabins otherwise we are going to get very confused. I know I will."

"How about tree names, we could have Mountain Ash, Grey Gum, and Iron Bark or you could have Bottlerush, Flame Tree and Ghost Gum. I can ask Terry to make up some name plaques from cut timber with his router. I think they would look good varnished."

"That's great and so simple, why didn't I think of that?" said Kat.

"Okay! Our cabin can be Mountain Ash. Number two cabin could be Iron bark and number three can be Flame Tree. I will ring Terry this morning and see if he can get on to making them up."

The day went quickly and after checking out number three cabin, they resumed the garden duties in Iron Bark. Katrina was right, both of the cabins were going to need everything new.

They came back early that afternoon because of a heavy rain shower, so they decided to go up to the main house and use the internet. Katrina thought if she could not physically work in the garden, she could at least set her mind on some paperwork and follow up some ordering.

She started checking out the online catalogues, so Zach left her and went in search of his family. His father was at his own computer, going through figures and his mother was out in the garden with some of the other pack members.

"Hey, Dad, Katrina is going through some of the ordering for the cabins, did you need anything?"

"No I think we're good. I am sure your mother did an order last week."

"Okay. Well we are replacing most of the smalls in both cabins, the furniture is still good. I am hoping that will be it but I have a feeling these are not the only cabins!"

"You guys may as well stay for dinner and we can discuss this more."

"No worries!"

"Zach, I need to talk to you about something when we are on our own."

"Do you need me to read it from you?"

"Yes, please, but I don't want it repeated."

Zach's eyes started to glow and he looked into his father's memory. He was suddenly aware of a picture Richard was portraying in his mind.

Richard was back in college and he was in a classroom. The teacher was talking about a book, so he guessed it must have been literature. In the classroom was Katrina's mother, Mary. She was young and pretty and very attractive with her black straight hair and emerald green eyes. He watched for a while and saw the class being dismissed for the afternoon. He watched his father walk out and Mary, too. They went their separate ways, but his father kept watching her. She had met her boyfriend who was quiet and withdrawn. He tried joking with her, but there was something wrong in his manner. Zach watched through his father's eyes as Mary and her boyfriend walked off through the woods to somewhere.

It looked like he was silently dragging her along and she did not look happy. It was getting darker, the further they were walking through the woods. The next part of his memory showed the couple were standing in the trees and the boyfriend arguing and had pulled out a knife to Mary's throat. Richard had appeared from nowhere and tackled the boyfriend and knocked him out. He then embraced Mary, who was screaming and very frightened. He used hypnosis on her to calm her down and to tell her to go back to school and leave the boyfriend there. He watched her walk away and then Richard's memory opened up into another window.

Mary was in another class and it was raining so Zach thought it must have been another day. There were some police officers, standing at the front of the class asking questions. Someone from the back shouted something about Mary and the policemen started to ask her questions.

She was getting distressed and crying, her boyfriend was missing, and she didn't know anything. Zach watched as his father walked over to comfort Mary. He rubbed her back and was explaining something to the police officers. They were writing it all down and left, never to return.

"Wow, that's heavy shit, Dad," Zach spoke inside Richard's head.

"Yes. I don't think she remembers the incident in the woods. Although what was strange about the whole thing was that her boyfriend was a shifter."

Katrina and Zach finished eating with the family and headed back to the cabin, when Zach asked, "What do you want to do now?"

"I would like to go for a ride!"

He looked at her and said, "In the truck? Didn't we just have one?"

"No! Silly," she said to him in her head. "I want you to take me for a ride?"

"Kat, you cannot be serious, I have never done it before and you are still sitting there with a broken leg. Anything could happen, you could fall off me, and I would never forgive myself."

"I trust you. I know you would never let anything happen to me, but I really want to do this!"

"Okay, but you will need to get dressed up with warm clothes."

Zach jumped up and went and found her a coat, he then placed a scarf around her neck and a hat on her head. Then he made sure she was warm before he picked her up and carried her outside, taking her to the veranda. He put her down on the cement path until he shimmered and turned into a beautiful griffin. He lowered himself down towards the ground for her to get on. He then helped her climb aboard his back, using his beak. Zach kept telling her in his head, that she really needed to hold on to his wings. He was so worried he just didn't like the idea at the moment, with her broken leg. She told him in her head that this is what she really wanted to do, she wanted to fly, end of story.

He took a sudden deep breath and then they took off, a rush of fresh air hitting her lungs. It was unbelievable; the sensation was nothing that could be at all possible in a human world.

They flew higher and higher up until he levelled out at a safe height. He made sure he was away from any chance of someone human, seeing them. All the time Katrina holding on to his wings for fear of falling. She knew for certain Zach would be reading her mind, and thinking he told her so! She braved herself and looked down and could see a few lights down on the ground, but she had no idea where they were. He circled around the mountain a couple of times and then came back to land near the cabin. As they landed she sat there, still shaking a little. He turned around and looked at her, his eyes glowing yellow.

"Are you okay?" he said in her head.

"Yes, I'm fine!"

"You don't look fine. You almost look like you are going to throw up!"

"Very funny," she said, smacking him on the side of his wing. "That was fantastic. I could never believe anything like that was possible."

"It would not be in your human world. Humans don't like to imagine things, let alone see anything at all strange, and they certainly would not discuss anything for worry of being marched off to a mental institution. Or what you would call the looney bin."

"Thanks, that makes me feel all warm and fuzzy."

He helped her climb down, only she ended up on her bottom. He burst out laughing, she felt a little foolish at first sitting on the cold grass. Only when she turned to see this creature with glowing eyes and an eagle head laughing at her, she, too, ended up laughing.

The next morning they had a visitor, Terry. He had come down with one of the plaques, *Iron Bark*, to show them. He had done a great job, using the best red cedar timber. It showed the different colours through the grain. The font he used to cut the name out could not have been better, they were really happy. He left, telling them he would start on the other two today and would see them tomorrow.

Richard seemed impressed with the work that had been carried out and said he might come down later with Amy for a visit.

Number three cabin, Rain Tree was in the same state as Iron Bark, (No.2) and would need at least the same amount of time to get it up to living standard. They decided they could also make a feature of the well as it was still in a good working order, although they would need to put a safety mesh barrier across the top, for insurance purposes. As they really didn't want any of their guests falling down the well and drowning.

Zach decided they would attach the next cabin once they had finished Iron Bark and then start on the trails.

"You do realise I will need to go back to work, once this plaster comes off next week? Even if it's to find a replacement nanny."

"I was hoping you would stay here?"

"I will, looks like I have plenty of work between here and the hotel, but I really cannot leave these people without a nanny! That would be totally unfair and mean."

"So what are you saying?"

"I am going to need to go back for a while, maybe a month or two, until I find a replacement who will look after the children. I mean properly, they need to know the children first, before they are aware of who they are working for. Otherwise you could get all sorts of Sheilas turning up, just for the chance to sleep with a rock star."

"That could take a while, and I don't want you away for that long!"

"Well, you will either have to come with me, or join me when you can."

Over the next week all three gardens had been cleaned up and the third cabin had been cleaned. A team of electricians had arrived from Charters Towers and were booked in to sort out all the cabins, by replacing any faulty wiring and any blown power points, light fittings and fans.

During a night flight Aaron and Craig had taken over the property, they had spotted another two cabins, so Richard had sent them up in the helicopter the next day to make sure there were no more.

At the end of the second week all cabins had been found and cleaned. They had cut a decent tractor path through the woodland to connect all five cabins together. Later they would need to clean all the branches away and make it safe for cars to drive down, unless they decided to drive guests to their cabin. There was a list of maintenance on each cabin that they would need to get through before the tourists' season started next year.

Richard was helping by designing the signs for 'The Black Boulders Retreat.' Amy had suggested that they update 'Thistle Ridges' as well and then there was no chance of guests getting lost or turning up at their home.

That evening they were having dinner up at the main house so Richard could go over a few things with Zach.

"I have ordered the signs, I thought we should put one of each of the signs at the beginning of the property and then again at the fork where you turn down to the boulders and one in town. Then we can make some arrow signs, using coppers logs, showing them into the retreat."

"That's good, Dad. We have nearly finished the landscaping. So when we take Katrina to Townsville to see the doctor for her next X-ray and hopefully the removal of her plaster, we can bring back some nursery plants."

"Katrina has also decided to go back to Brisbane."

"Only until I can find a suitable nanny to take my place, Zach. Besides, all my clothes and belongings are down there. Not to mention my laptop and books."

"Do you think that is wise?" Richard said.

"Why don't you think it's wise, Richard?" Kat asked.

"Well, there's nobody to guard you down there."

"Why do I need guarding? I am just going to be inside most of the time."

"Because you and Zach are together, and Zach is a griffin shifter. He is one of the rarest shifters in the world, so if someone wanted to get to him, they would pick a fight with you first. You are only human and not very strong at all, so I couldn't expect you to defend yourself.

"Thanks, I am really touched."

"Katrina, you are a Williams now so you need to protect yourself."

"Well what about Abbey, she's still down there working. Shouldn't she be back here as well?"

"Yes, that is true. Aaron needs to go down to claim her and then bring her back here," Richard said.

"But why don't I go down with Aaron? I can pack all my stuff and advertise for a nanny. Aaron can try and sort Abbey out. Good luck with that, by the way – and maybe all come home together."

"What do you mean, sis?" Aaron said.

"You will find out, but I will let you into a little secret. Abbey and I left this tiny little town to get our independence and to live in the city. That's all we ever wanted to do, the city life called us. So you'd better have a good plan to entice her back here or she won't come."

The whole table went quiet; you could hear everyone's brains ticking.

"What about the trail rides? Would she be happy doing that with you?" Aaron asked.

"She's good at breaking horses in and training them. She might be!" Kat said

"Okay! It's getting late, people, let's think about this over the next few days and see what comes up," Richard said as he got up from the table.

"I want to go home, Zach. I don't want to stay here any more. Give me your automatic truck and I will see you tomorrow."

"Honey, you don't have to do this. Dad was only trying to explain what was best for us all."

"Oh yes, I bloody do! Give me the damn bloody keys before I start walking."

"Here, take them. Do you want me to drop you off?"

"No, I don't. Just leave me alone and let me have some bloody air."

"Let me at least put you in the truck."

"Fine."

She started the motor and Zach watched as she took off down the driveway. He went back inside to see his brothers and both parents standing in the kitchen, looking worried and waiting for him.

"Sorry, son. I was only trying to put safety first. We don't want anything happening to her."

"She might be tiny, but look out, Zach, she's got a good fiery temper to go with that hair," Craig said.

They all laughed, but they were also worried about her.

The hotel was still open when she drove in half an hour later. She hobbled out and found her father in the bar.

"Hello, Katrina. Is everything all right, with you, honey?" he said as he pulled back a bar chair and picked her up and sat her down. Like when she was seven.

"No, I have just had a big fight with Zach's family, mainly Richard so I have come home."

"Good for you honey, you sit up here and tell me all about it," Charlie said. "Can I fix you a drink? You really look like you need one?"

"Yes, please, Dad. I will have a glass of red wine."

"Coming up. Did you just drive yourself here?"

"Yes. I got Zach's automatic. Lucky I broke my leg, otherwise I would still have been there."

Charlie turned around suddenly, remembering his manners, and introduced Katrina to some guests who had booked in and were staying overnight. They were sitting in the corner at one of the tables with a map spread out in front of them.

"Mr and Mrs Donahue book a couple of nights with us every year. On their way up to Cairns and on the way back to Melbourne. They have been up to visit their daughter."

"Wow, you have travelled quite a way. That must be at least a four-day drive to here, without travelling to Cairns," Kat said.

"Pleased to meet you. Yes, it takes us at least six days to travel from Melbourne up to Cairns," Mr Donahue said as he got up from their table and came across to shake Katrina's hand.

"My daughter has broken her leg, but is itching to get back to Brisbane," Charlie said.

"Well, if you need a lift, we will be leaving early in the morning," Mrs Donohue said.

"Thanks for the offer but I need to get this leg X-rayed in Townsville tomorrow or the next day, and then I can get this stupid cast off."

"Okay. Well, if you change your mind, just let your dad know," Mr Donohue said.

"Okay, I will, thanks," Katrina said.

Mr Donohue returned to his seat and after speaking with his wife, started to pack up their things. They left soon after, saying their goodnights, leaving just Kat and her father in the bar. She had another glass of wine while he packed away the till for the night.

"Zach wants to marry me, and he wants me to come back here. But I cannot leave the children without a nanny. I feel obliged to go back and help them until we can find a replacement. I have been with them since before Alex was born, looking after Martha."

"Well I am sure Zach must understand that. Did you talk to him?"

"Not exactly. Richard was telling us what he thought would be better. Zach was just agreeing to what his dad was saying. I was getting more and more pissed off, you know how I hate being told what to do."

"Yes, I do. It must be something in that red hair ah!"

"Anyway, all my belongings are down there. So the suitable plan would be to go back and hire a nanny. Train her and then pack up all my stuff and come home," Kat said, fighting the tears back. "I don't know why everyone is being so weird."

"Well maybe you should have a little time away from him. Then you can decide what you really want to do. I know for one, your mother and I would be very happy to have you back here. We miss you!"

"Did someone mention my name?"

"Hey, Mum."

"Hello! Darling, you been having troubles? I just got off the phone from Amy. She told me you left after a heated argument and she was worried sick about you."

"Wow, that didn't take long! I just needed to get away."

"Zach has asked her to marry him, and he and the family want her to come back to town permanently," Charlie said.

"I said I would, in my own time. This is why I liked my freedom. I didn't have to worry about any one."

"Well maybe you can ring him tomorrow and sort this all out? I am sure it can't be that bad."

"Okay!" Kat said as she hugged her mother.

Charlie and Mary helped Katrina up the stairs and walked the little journey to her bedroom.

"Don't worry any more about it now, honey, I am sure Zach will be here to sort everything out in the morning. You are far too important to lose and he knows that," Charlie said.

"Thanks, Dad. I hope you are right. I do love him but why does it have to be so hard?" Kat said.

"Love is never easy," Mary said.

"If you are still determined to go to Townsville tomorrow, I can ask Barney to give you a lift. He's coming through in the morning with his truck, delivering my beer order," Charlie said.

"Okay! That would be great. I have not been on a road train in years. Thanks, Dad."

"We will see you in the morning. Love you, Katrina," her mother said as she kissed her good night.

"See you for breakfast, Katrina, and I love you too," Charlie said giving her a bear hug.

"Love you too guys."

She went over to her cupboard and pulled out her suitcase, and started to throw her clothes on the bed that she had brought from Brisbane and never used. She had always been comfortable in jeans, but had some lovely dresses if needed for special occasions. With the exception of old clothes that she used for mustering and the clothes she had left out at Zach's, everything was packed.

She hobbled into the bathroom and strapped her leg up before climbing into the shower and letting the hot water warm her aching body. She could not believe her life was suddenly so complicated.

There was a knock at the window as she climbed out of the shower. So after drying herself off and putting a comb through her hair, she walked slowly over to the window and looked out through the curtains. There, looking back at her, was her beautiful griffin. He was perched on top of the flat roof of the garages. She opened the window, ready for another fight, but nothing happened. Instead she was asked how she was feeling, in her head. He could tell how badly she was hurting and wanted to make it right.

She climbed out on to the window sill, holding on tightly to her towel, and edged her way onto the roof. Never in all her days growing up as a child had she ever ventured out on to this roof. She moved cautiously along the roof, not wanting to fall and hurt herself. He never took his eyes off her, until she was standing right in front of him. Katrina buried her head in his neck amongst the pile of soft feathers and started to cry. He really wanted to shift and hold her tight to him and comfort her. But he thought better of it as his griffin was also crying out for her, wanting to embrace her. As if knowing, at that moment Kat brought her arms up and reached around his neck. The griffin very gently brought his wing around to hold her and protect her from the cool air. She didn't know how long she had stood there, wrapped up in his warm wing, but she was feeling a little better. She walked back to the window sill and climbed into her room without saying another word. She had already told him what she had decided to do, and he would have to like it. Or she wasn't ready to a whole commitment.

Zach fluffed up his feathers and started to shimmer back. She was still angry at him, but not his beautiful griffin, she loved that side of him. But she was finding it was hard to be angry when he was wearing just a pair of tight jeans and nothing else. All she could see was rippling muscles and tight abs that she wanted to run her fingers over. He started to walk towards her and became a little shocked when she put up a hand signalling a stop!

"I might only be twenty-two but I am a smart woman. So when someone tells me to do something, I don't like. It normally makes me more determined not to do it. You ask my father; he will tell you. I know your dad means well, but I am not used to your way of life.

"Tomorrow I want to go to Townsville get this stupid bloody thing off my leg and then I am going to get a flight back to Brisbane."

He walked towards her and wiped the tears from her cheeks away. He had never loved any one so much in his life. He kissed her softly on the mouth and hugged her into his body. She brought her arms up and touched his face.

"I truly love you with all my heart, but I don't think I am ready. This is moving too fast and it scares the hell out of me."

"Okay. We can slow down a little if you want and I will speak to my father tomorrow. See if he can give us some more time?"

"Thank you," she said.

She pulled his head down to kiss him gently on the lips and feeling her heart beat a little too fast, he walked her over to the bed. He picked up the side of her bedding and opened it for her to slide in. Zach gently pulled her wet towel down and kissed her neck. He then covered her with the sheet and doona and sat down beside her.

"I will not lose you, Katrina. I love you too much, – my griffin loves you as well – to have some little problem like this break us apart.

"Are you sure you are ready to travel? You are still going to need to rest that leg."

"Oh! I am sure. I need time away from here to make up my mind what I want to do. Your family are so demanding and I will not be pushed into anything."

"Well, if you are so determined to go back to Brisbane, I will take you myself."

He kissed her on the lips and got up and moved towards the window. She really thought he was going to go and she called out to him. He turned, looking at her with his eyes glowing.

"Please don't go like this. I don't want you to leave. I promise not to argue any more."

He walked back but his eyes were still glowing. He dropped his jeans by the side of the bed and the climbed in beside her. They were both naked and it sent a thrill up her spine. He slid over to her and then covered her with his body. Resting on his elbows he was just leaning over her looking down at her. She was so turned on that she pulled his head towards her and kissed him on the mouth. She prised his mouth open with her tongue and then started to lick the inside of his mouth and suck his lips. He moved slightly to the side and used one hand to massage her breasts. He then took the closest one and sucked it hard. She squirmed a little at the sensation hardening her nipples and making her throb between her thighs. She wanted him so badly and told him, but he was not listening. Instead he pulled her legs apart and moved down her body, kissing and sucking her skin. He moved down to the top of her thighs and inserted a finger into her folds and then another one. She cried out from pleasure. He moved his fingers in and out until she was arching her back for more. He bent down and licked her clit until she was rocking violently with an orgasm. After her climax had worn off a little he climbed back over her and pushed his hard length into her wet entry.

She cried out with his fullness but also from the pleasure it was giving her. Her whole body was pulsating as Zach was driving in and out with his body. Suddenly the griffin wanted out, he needed his mate, too. It seemed like Zach was losing a little control and she was aware that the griffin was wanting her as much as Zach did. She found he was suddenly getting a little rougher but not enough to worry about. He pushed deeper and deeper until he exploded his seed in her. Her body shuddered and exploded as she hit another orgasm that left her breathless and numb all over.

She was still breathing hard as Zach's eyes came back to normal.

"I am sorry about that if I was a little rough and hurt you, it was not my intention. My griffin wanted to get out and he seemed to need you as well. After the threat of losing you today, he was getting a little hard to control," he said kissing her neck and earlobe.

"It's all right, I'm fine. My body won't work for me but I am good. I don't think I have ever had such great sex," she said, laughing.

Zach encircled her into his chest with his strong arms protecting her and that's where she slept all night, until he needed to get up, and leave before daylight approached.

Chapter 7

At the crack of dawn, Aaron, Craig and Zach pulled into the car park of the hotel. They were climbing out of the vehicle when they noticed some guests leaving. An alert went up through Zach's spine and his griffin sensors were telling him to be wary. All three of them stopped dead in their tracks and watched as the guests from the hotel climbed into their four-wheel drive. They all stood there until the car disappeared down the street followed by a large caravan.

"Morning," said Charlie as he held the front door open for them.

"Morning Charlie, the boys just dropped me off so I can take Katrina to Townsville."

Charlie didn't need to know that Zach stayed the night and only flew home this morning, before it got light.

"Hey, Charlie. Who were your guests?" Craig asked.

"It's Mr and Mrs Donohue. They come every year for a visit here in town. Mrs Donohue particularly likes to stop for a bit of gold fossicking and sightseeing. They stay for a couple of days on the way through, and on their return home to Melbourne. Mr and Mrs Donohue travel up north along the East Coast road to Cairns. They said they have a daughter up there, working in one of the large schools. Seem very nice, they offered to give Katrina a lift back to Brisbane. She was so upset when she returned last night, she seemed so determined about wanting to go back to work."

Zach took off at a full gallop, past Charlie and up the stairs, around the corner to the staff quarters. He flew in through the door and was relieved to see Katrina just coming out of the shower.

"Oh! Thank the gods. I thought, for a minute ..." He ran straight to her and grabbed her into a strong embrace.

Hugging her body tightly, into his strong chest. His heart was racing, and his eyes were a fierce golden colour. He was still standing like that, when his brothers came rushing in.

"Is she all right?" Aaron said.

"Zach, is she safe?" Craig called out from the bedroom door.

"Yes, she's here, just came walking out of the shower. With no idea of what has been going on."

She looked up at Zach, whose eyes were still glowing and then to his brothers, confused. Standing still, encircled in Zach's arms, she was dripping water everywhere, holding on to the tiniest towel wrapped around her petite frame.

She moved her arms around his waist because she could feel his heart beating so fast, she needed to calm him down.

"It's all right, Zach I am here. Whatever is wrong? Everything is fine," she said kissing his cheek and then his lips.

"Nice towel, sis." Kat could feel a small vibration starting in her chest and suddenly the vibrating got louder until there was growling. It was only then she remembered the growling in the bar. It was Zach; he was protecting her, his mate. Brother or no brother, Aaron had over stepped the boundaries.

"Aaron! That's my mate you are looking at. Please have a little respect."

"Sorry, so sorry!" he said, trying to stop himself from laughing.

"Maybe you and Craig could order some breakfast for all of us. While Katrina gets herself ready, or you could go and check out the room the Donahues where using."

"I want to know everything about them and why my sensors were going off. Now go!"

They rushed out of the room and closed the door fast. He could hear them running down the hallway to the stairs.

He stood back a little and took some deep breaths whilst his eyes stopped glowing gold. He was still a little shaky as Kat's arms came up and circled his neck. She pulled him down to her height and kissed him on the lips.

"He meant no harm. He says what I would expect Jared to say," Kat whispered. "What's really going on, and don't cover up like you have been. I want the truth, or this relationship is not going to last."

"Okay the guests that were staying here last night, Donahues. Well we met them downstairs and my sensors went off alerting me to danger. When your father said that they had offered you a lift back to Brisbane, I had this horrible feeling that they might have kidnapped you. We all freaked and that's why we all rushed in here like mad men. We think they are shifters but I don't know why I am sensing danger. It only makes me worry more about you. Now we have to make up something to tell your father."

"Don't worry, he will be fine. I told him last night that you want to marry me."

"You did? How did that go? They would love me to come home, they really like you and your family. They like the whole idea of what you are doing out at Thistle Ridge."

"I have repacked my case this morning, leaving nearly everything here. So when I pack down in Brisbane I won't have all these clothes to bring back again, making more work."

"There's only one thing wrong with that."

"What?" she said looking straight into his beautiful eyes.

"They are not hanging in my closet."

Zach let Katrina finish getting dressed and after a while both made their way downstairs, Zach helping Katrina down the steep stairs and then running back up to collect her luggage.

They followed the laughter of his brothers down the hallway to the kitchen. Craig had taken over the toaster and Aaron was making coffee. Katrina's parents were busy plating up some bacon and eggs.

"I knew you guys would come in handy for something," Zach said.

He looked at his brothers and smiled, trying to apologise. They both dropped their heads in acknowledgement and carried on like nothing had happened. Only Katrina noticed they were bowing down to him.

They all sat down for breakfast in the dining room and made small talk.

"So Charlie, while my brothers are here, I would like to ask you if I could have your daughter's hand in marriage."

Charlie coughed, his toast going down the wrong way. Mary smiled Aaron nearly split his coffee and Katrina and Craig burst out laughing. Suddenly everyone was looking at Zach.

"What?"

"You could have asked him after we'd finished breakfast, and then we're not choking to death," said Aaron.

"Sorry, but I wanted to get it out in the open. You know, do the right thing," said Zach

"It's fine, Zach, It's only been six or seven weeks that you to have been together. But I can see you are both in love so I give you my blessing and Mary's too. No plans for a quick wedding, are there?"

"No, sir. There's certainly no reason to be rushing. I just want to let everyone that she is my girlfriend and now fiancée. We're both quite happy to wait a while. Aren't we, Katrina?"

"Yes, we are happy to wait. No babies, if that's what you're thinking, Dad. I think next spring sounds good to me for a wedding. I will be twenty-three then. Might make it a double wedding, if Aaron ever gets his act together."

"Ha! Ha! Sis. You really are comical; I think we might be on a wager there."

"Okay! How much are you talking?"

"I say $50.00 says you can't manage it."

"That's all you got, sis?"

"Okay! Let's make it $100.00. Double wedding next spring. You can even pick the bloody date."

"You're on!"

They both stood up and shook hands, leaving everyone around the table shaking their heads.

They said their goodbyes after breakfast, Katrina hugging her parents, promising she would ring them as soon as they got to Townsville and after she had seen the doctor. Hopefully with good news of her leg. She would also ring them again when they arrived in Brisbane, as they always worried so much when she was travelling.

Aaron headed back to Thistle Ridge in one car leaving Craig to jump into the back seat of Zach's truck, which Katrina had driven back last night in her temper. Katrina climbed into the front seat, with Zach's help. Once the luggage had been loaded they drove off.

Once they were on their way Zach asked his brother if they had found anything in the Donahues' room.

"There was a real stink in the room. I have never smelt it before, but I would say wet dog."

"Holy shit, you think they are werewolves? They have been coming past this way for years."

"No one has noticed because they have always mingled with humans."

"Do you think they'll know about us now?"

"I think we have just made it known, by the way we were all standing our ground. Protecting our new territory. If they were shifters they will know we were too."

"That's what I was afraid of, but we are living here now. So we will need to make a stand," Zach said.

"Better ring and fill Dad in."

Craig got his phone out and hit a button. Katrina was looking a little worried and moved her hand over to Zach's lap. He squeezed her hand and kissed the back of it.

"Don't worry, we will sort this out, they might just be genuine. As your father said, they have been travelling along these roads for years. Not expecting to meet any other shifters out this far west."

Craig was in the back, talking and then listening. Zach could hear his father yelling something down the phone. He put the phone down and let out a big sigh.

"Father said he will ask his friend in the police force to run a check on their car plates, to see if they are who they say they are. Also to get a real address off the registration and to see if any werewolves are registered as living in that town. He told me to stay with you, at all costs and that Aaron will fly the helicopter to Townsville and pick us up there. He has suggested, but really told me, that he wants us all to go to Brisbane. He will speak to Abbey's dad, but he wants the two girls back here under pack protection. He has given us a week, maybe two at the most. In that time we will need to pack them both up, find a replacement for Katrina's work, and then bring everyone home safe and sound."

"They will both need protecting now they are mates to two royal family heirs. Whether they like it or they don't. They are both too precious to lose," Craig said.

"Okay! Well, that seems pretty final, Katrina. Howe-ver, I did manage to talk to him this morning and he was happy for us to take some time as you were not a shifter and did not understand the rules we abide by."

"Well, that was very generous of him," Kat said through gritted teeth.

"I am sorry now that I brought you into the shifters' world. But you will need to take our relationship seriously. We are not human and there are bad shifters and people out there, who would do anything for money," Zach said.

"Okay! I see that now. I will ring Rob when we get to Townsville and let him know what's happening. I will make up something about having to come home permanently for family reasons or something."

Two hours later they pulled into Charters Towers, only to stop at a service station to buy some takeaway coffees. Kat was still very quiet, and deep in her own thoughts. Wondering how and why life had suddenly become such a mess and dangerous all of a sudden. Two months ago she knew nothing of this shifter world. She didn't believe in fairy tales when Martha asked if there were fairies and dragons. Now she just didn't know what to believe.

She had decided last night after everything that she was committed to the relationship with Zach and could never live without him. Leaving nothing to do but surrender to him and his family. She was pissed but there did not seem to be any way out of it.

One and a half hours later they arrived in Townsville. Zach drove up to the entrance of the hospital and parked at the drop off area. To let Katrina climbed out, Zach jumped out and collected her crutches from the back of the truck.

They walked up to the huge front glass doors and went inside. They made their way to the information centre to find out where they could find Kat's doctor. Craig went and parked the car saying he would catch up with them in a while.

The appointment was in an hour so they went to the café and bought some lunch. Katrina had managed to get in to see her doctor as there had been a cancellation. Otherwise she would have had to wait another day.

"I know what you're thinking and it's too late. That if you go back to Brisbane, and leave me at Twin Hills, you might be all right. I have claimed you as my mate, if you did not see me for a month or more you would still smell of me. Not to a human, but to a shifter and I would never forgive myself if anything happened to you."

"I know, but I just was so settled in my job. I had my own unit attached to Rob's huge house, so I could be away from the rest of the house and still keep a little independence. I loved working with the kids, and we had fun. I also didn't mind flying around the world in private jets, visiting countries that I could never have afforded, let alone the experience. It was the high life I always wanted. I had dreamed about since I was a kid, and now in a matter of two months I am going home again."

"Katrina, I am so sorry, I don't know how many times I can tell you that."

"It's all right, Zach. It's just going to take me some time. I really was not expecting it to happen to me that's all. Who would have thought I would find love in a place I was not thinking of ever returning to?"

"What about your parents' hotel? Didn't you want to take that over later?"

"Maybe! When I am fifty something years old."

"Well, you won't be bored; there will always be the cabins and the tourists. If you take on the horse rides that will keep you busy, and I am sure I can find you lots of other things to do! When we're all alone, that is."

She laughed and pulled his hand into her lap. He picked up her hand and kissed it.

"I really am sorry, you know that, don't you?"

"Yes, I know."

'Come on let's find your doctor."

After her X-ray showed the bone had welded itself back together. The doctor was happy to take the plaster off her leg. He asked her to keep a support bandage for a week or two, until the strength came back in her leg muscles and ankle, and she was free to go.

They caught up with Craig at the front of the hospital, talking to someone on his phone.

He did not look very happy and reached in his pocket to give Zach the car keys. They all walked back to the car and headed to the airport.

"That was Dad. He said that Aaron should be nearly at the airport to pick us up. We just need to park the car in long term parking and he will arrive at gate 3."

Zach stopped at the passenger drop off point, outside the departure lounge and went inside the building to find a trolley for their luggage.

He let Craig drive off and go to find the long-term car park, while he helped Katrina hobble in to the departure lounge. Gate 3 was quite a walk away from the main tourist areas of cafés and souvenir shops. It was found on the far side of the airport building away from all the main stream traffic of the busy runway.

"Have you managed to think what you are going to say to Rob, about us all coming down?"

"No! Wouldn't it be better if Aaron and Craig went to stay with Abbey?"

"Well if it's not too far away, I just had a thought. Don't you think Abbey and Aaron are going to want some alone time, like we did? Poor Craig is going to feel like a spare wheel, where ever he goes."

Katrina pulled out her old phone and showed Zach on a GPS map where Abbey lived and where they were going to be.

"You might be right; does Abbey know we're coming back?"

"I'll text her."

"I am sure Aaron would have contacted her by now."

It was not long before they saw the helicopter come in to land. They could see Aaron was busy, talking to the guy with the small refuelling tanker. Katrina decided to ring Rob and let him know they were coming back. She also needed check if it was all right that she brought her fiancé back with her. He didn't seem to mind at all, when she told him that she'd only gotten the plaster taken off that morning and she still needed a little help getting around. He was just happy that she was at last coming back. He told her he could let his mother go home now, as she was driving him nuts.

When she put the phone down Aaron was walking up the gang way to them.

"Hey long time no see, brother, little sister."

"Everything all right with your flight here? No problems with refuelling?"

"No, all good. I have spoken to Abbey and we are going to meet up later. She's not happy at all, she wanted to give the hospital at least a month's notice, not a week. Her contract says she needs to give at least two weeks' notice so Dad is going to have to go with that."

"I have just spoken to Rob, and let him know we are coming today. I told him my plaster only came off today. That's why you are coming with me because I still need help to get around. I did not tell him anything else. I will talk to him when we get there."

"Do we have a plan?" Zach asked.

"Well from here we can fly directly in to Brisbane. Once we arrive at the airport we will need a car to get us around the city. Unless you girls have cars?"

"Abbey doesn't have one, but I do. It's only a little Pulsar, but it's nippy. You can use mine to get around, but I am not sure if all three of you will fit?"

"Humour, sis, I like that," Aaron said.

"We are also going to need to hire a small removal truck to pick up all of Abbey's furniture, if she wants to take it back to Twin Hills. Unless of course, she wants to sell it. We still have to work out her lease for her unit, with the real-estate. She might be able to sub-let it to one of the other nurses. Otherwise we are going to have to pay rent until her lease is up. After sorting out all of this, then we start on Katrina's things," Aaron said.

"Your dad thinks we are going to be able to do all this in a fortnight?" Kat asked.

"It's a freaking nightmare!" Zach said.

They waited until Craig joined them and then went down to the helicopter. After luggage had been stowed away safely in the back, they climbed in and waited for clearance from the command tower.

After watching two army jets come in to land they received the all clear from the tower to leave. With headsets on and everyone strapped in, they took off into the sky, heading south to Brisbane.

Several hours later, Zach moved Katrina lightly to wake her up. She was startled and amazed with all the noise of the flight, that she had actually fallen asleep. Kat looked around to see that Aaron had already parked the helicopter and was outside covering up its blades. After all the checks were finalized with the ground crew, they headed inside the airport.

It was a much larger airport, being the capital of Queensland, and very busy. Katrina had lost count of all the gates, for domestic and international flights at forty something. She was suddenly feeling tired and wishing she had asked the brothers to hire a wheelchair. When she stopped to catch her breath, as if feeling her pain, Zach stopped past the trolley to Craig and picked her up. She circled her arms around his neck and kissed his cheek.

"You're a good man, have I told you that today?"

"Sorry, I should have thought it was too long a journey for your leg," Zack said. At last they found the car hire booths and proceeded to the least busy one. Aaron and Craig filled in all the paper work needed to hire the car. Then they were all moving again. Katrina helped Aaron put their addresses into the NAV man GPS and then they made their way out of the airport. Heading to Rob's first, at Charles Avenue and then on to Abbey's.

Katrina rang and spoke to Rob to let him know they were arriving soon. He told her he would leave the main security gates open at the front of the property, that way making it easier for her to get in. They had set the GPS and it took them straight there without any problems.

When they drove in to the large circular driveway, Katrina heard a whistle from the front seat. The house certainly had the wow factor and stood back in all its glory. Surrounded by picturesque trees and manicured lawns, it had always reminded Katrina of the film *Gone with the Wind*. It had at least three floors, with six large glass windows on each floor. The two centre windows on the second floor had a large concrete balcony extending out and underneath there were six huge white concrete columns holding it up. Each side of the steps leading up to the entrance accommodated miniature fig trees in large terracotta pots.

"Man, this place is crawling with money. What did you say he did, sis?"

"I told you he was a lead singer in a rock band and he's very nice too, so be polite," Katrina said to Craig and Aaron.

"Yeah, whatever, sis," Aaron barked.

"Aaron you really need to get laid. You are so uptight and cranky."

"Katrina, I don't believe you just said that to my brother," said Craig.

Zach was also looking at Kat, but he had an amused look on his face. He was looking at her like he had approved of the banter that she was giving her new brother.

Once they stopped and got out of the car the front door opened and the butler came out.

"Welcome back, Miss Katrina, how lovely to see you," said Miles.

Katrina walked over to Miles and gave him a hug. There was a low rumbling growl, which she ignored, from Zach.

"Thanks Miles, it is certainly nice to be back. Everything looks wonderful in the gardens. Looks like you have been having some good weather here in Brisbane?"

"Yes we have had perfect weather for at least two weeks now. The gardeners have been busy putting in all the annuals for summer and mowing."

Miles would have been close to sixty years old, so Kat could not understand why Zach was growling. Poor Miles looked around, thinking he was hearing things. He decided it was his imagination and led them all in to the house. As they walked into the mansion they were greeted with a large timber-clad hallway, covered in colourful paintings and tapestries, with polished cream and beige marble flooring and a carved polished oak table standing in the middle. There were two rooms on either side of the hall and a huge timber staircase going up to the first floor. When you looked further up past the first floor, the stairs split and went in two different directions, one to the left and the other to the right. It certainly was amazing.

Miles ushered them all into the large day room near the main entrance, on the right. Saying he would return with refreshments. Five minutes later Miles returned with a tray of sandwiches and hot mugs of coffee. It was welcomed by now as they were all hungry and thirsty.

Katrina could hear a little voice and looked up to see Rob coming into the room with Martha. She jumped up, putting her coffee down, just in time to see the little three-year-old running and squealing towards her. Katrina picked her up and squeezed her tightly.

"God, I have missed you, little one."

They stood hugging each other for a while until Rob came over. He gave her a half pat on the back and a small hug welcoming her back. Feeling a little intimidated from the three large men, or shifters, who had arrived in his home.

"Rob, this is Zach, and his brothers, Craig and Aaron. Guys, this is my boss, Rob."

They all got up and walked over to meet Rob and shake his hand.

"You have a lovely place here," said Aaron.

"Thank you. We like it, don't we Martha?" he said.

"Katrina, how is your leg now? It must have been a horrible experience for you. Lying there under that huge horse for hours, in the middle of nowhere and wondering if help was coming. We are so glad you are on the mend and have nearly recovered," Rob said.

"Yes, we missed you, Rina," said Martha. Katrina laughed and put her down.

"I am good, thanks, Rob. I just need to build my leg muscles back up. Which I am sure I can do chasing Martha around."

"I must have missed you telling me you had a boyfriend. I would have given you a little more time off," Rob said.

"It was all very sudden, a holiday romance with a twist, I think you could say," Kat said.

Miles walked in and made his way up to Rob and announced that he had a telephone call. Rob excused himself from the gathering and told Katrina he would catch up with them later, if he could get away.

"Okay! Well, we might go as well. It's Craig's turn to buy the beers at the pub. I think Abbey should have finished her shift now at the hospital," Aaron said, looking at Zach.

They were both staring at each other and listening to something. It must have been too far away, because Katrina couldn't hear anything. She got up to walk to the door with Martha and still could not hear a thing.

The three brothers followed her out of the room just as a lady in her late fifties early sixties was heading down the huge stair case.

She was dressed immaculately, wearing a pin stripe suit and high heels. Her blonde hair was scraped back in a tight bun, making her look a lot older than she probably was.

"There you are, Martha, I was wondering where you were. Hello, Katrina, welcome home."

"Hello, Mrs Saunders, I hope the children have not been too much for you."

"No dear, I love being around them. How is your leg now?"

"It's on the mend, thank you. I just won't be able to run for a while. So hopefully Martha will be good."

"I told Robert I would stay around for another week to help you settle in."

"Oh, thank you, that is kind but I bought back some help. This is my partner Zach. Zach this is Robert's Mother, Mrs Saunders." Zach waited for her to finish walking down the stairs and step into the hall, before going over to meet her and to shake her hand.

"These are Zach's younger brothers, Craig and Aaron. We all travelled back to Brisbane together. They were just leaving."

"Well, you don't have to run off on my account. It's nice having the house full of people you should all stay for dinner. It would be nice to have friends here, instead of just Robert and myself."

"Maybe we could do it during the week, once everyone gets settled in to where they're staying?" Kat asked.

"That sounds good. Come on, Martha we need to get you ready for bed. Then I think Cook's got your favourite for tea."

"See you, Rina," Martha said and followed her grandmother back up the stairs.

"See you tomorrow, cutie."

Chapter 8

Katrina gave Zach a quick tour of the house on their way to the back of the property to her private accommodation. Katrina, Miles and Sheila, the cook, were employed full time and lived on the property, whereas the gardeners and the maintenance crew came in twice a week, if needed.

They all had small town houses which at some time had been part of the main house. Whoever had updated the property had done a good job in sealing off the original eight rooms on the two floors and turning them into town houses, adding an open timber staircase in each house taking you up to a large bedroom and en-suite upstairs, whilst downstairs, the builders had made it all open plan, leaving a good-sized living room and a dining room attached to the kitchenette. Robert had supplied his employees with a large TV and DVD player when they were off duty.

A decent size futon that could be converted into a double bed if any of them had guests to stay overnight. An internal phone system, where they could be reached at any time and Katrina also had child monitors set up so she could hear the children at night.

They walked in to find Miles had already been in and left their luggage by the bottom of the staircase. They made their way over to the lounge and sat down, Katrina kicking off her sneakers.

"This is my little home away from Twin Hills home. I love it here because it's all mine and I can please myself. I can watch whatever TV channel I want to. I can watch girlie films with no one watching me, or to laugh at me if I cry, because it's sad."

"I would never laugh at you. I adore you."

Katrina pulled his head down and kissed him lightly on the lips. She moved her hands up under his shirt, just as his phone rang.

"Yes? What's happening?"

"Okay. We have arrived at Abbey's place and she's home. There's plenty of room for Craig, so there is no drama with putting him up. We have made a booking at the pizza restaurant around the corner from where you guys are for 7pm. Kat will know where to go. See you then."

Aaron hung up the phone before Zach could say anything.

"Well, it looks like we are going out to dinner. There's a pizza place around the corner. It's booked for 7pm so we have time for a quick shower."

"Right then, I will go first."

Katrina moved and Zach grabbed her around the waist.

"What was the rest of that conversation, little one?"

Kat went pink in the face and looked at him.

"I was going to say, that I might need mine cold because what I had planned is going to have to wait until we come back."

They arrived at the pizza restaurant and waited to be seated. There was no sign of the others so they must be caught in traffic or something. The waitress sat them at the reserved table and took their drinks order.

"So are you going to tell what you have planned?" asked Zach.

"No! I am sorry but I don't disclose secrets. You will have to – oh, lovely, thank you," she said as the waitress put down their glasses of wine. Zach laughed and grabbed her hand as the others arrived at the table. Abbey rushed over and gave Katrina a big hug.

"God, I have missed you. Is everything alright?" Abbey said.

"You mean, apart from having to give up your once in a lifetime job. To give up flying in private jets, like royalty. To stop going to different countries, all over the world and stay in their exquisite hotels, as part of the job. To go home to the small town I have always hated. Only to move in with some hot, sexy, god-like creature of a man. Yeah I'm good."

The whole table was laughing; Abbey gave her another hug and went and sat down next to Aaron.

"I could say the same, but my job is not as exciting as yours," Abbey said

"Yes, but you do go home like me and live with a sexy man as well." She could hear Zach quietly growling.

"Yes you are right about that, I just have not seen him naked yet!" Abbey said.

"I am right here, girls," said Aaron.

She looked over at Zach and scowled at him, shutting him up. She said to him without talking, "This is going to be normal banter between brothers and sisters so you had better get used to it." Directing her conversation back to Abbey, she asked, "Maybe we could have a small hospital built for you in Twin Hills? I am sure we are going to need one if the town grows any bigger."

"No I am all right, I'll help you sort out these riding stables and break in some horses for the tourist season next year. I can always go back to nursing if this does not work out" Abbey said laughing.

"Hey, like I said before, I am right here!" Aaron said, leaning over and kissing Abbey.

The waitress came and took their order and then came back with some more wine for Katrina and Zach and lager for the rest of them. The girls ordered chicken Caesar salad, while the brothers ordered pizzas, lasagne and side salads. The conversation turned back to Twin Hills.

"Did we find out any more on the guests at the hotel?" asked Zach.

"Yes, we did, the plates were legitimate and registered in the Donohue name. The home address seems to be real as well. They are just going to check out the mailing system to make sure. It might be the right address but whether they live there is a different matter."

"Good work. Anything else?" asked Zach

The meal arrived and stopped the conversation for a while until the waitress left.

"There seems to be something happening with Katrina's boss. That phone call we heard today, it seems like he is in some legal battle with an old manager. The manager was sacked after he stopped supplying the band with enough gigs. Even though he was on a lot of commission, he seemed to be spending more time with some girl band."

"Well, after a couple of weeks that won't be our problem," said Craig.

"Katrina has not given her notice in yet. She was going to see him tonight," said Zach.

"I still don't think we can be out of here in two weeks. Maybe three would be better. Your father will just have to sit tight and wait," Kat said, watching Aaron and Craig nearly choke.

"I second that! I still have to sub lease my apartment, as it doesn't come up for renewal for another seven months. I have to pack up all my belongings and work my two weeks' notice," said Abbey.

"Okay. Well, if we need more time I will talk to Father, but I don't like the idea."

They spent the rest of the meal chatting and making small talk. Katrina and Abbey were talking about a few plans they could work on when they returned to Thistle Ridge.

Zach went off to settle the bill and came back to Craig and Aaron's side. He said something very quietly and they both went on high alert.

The atmosphere of their party suddenly changed and there was tension in the air. The five of them stayed close together and walked outside. Zach and Aaron pushed slightly in front, protecting their mates. As they were walking to their cars they noticed someone standing in the shadows. Zach started growling and his sensors were going off, telling him to shift, but they were in a popular eating area, with humans all around them.

Out of the shadows walked a couple of men, and behind them they could see at least another four. They made their way over to Zach's party.

Zach was trying to determine whether they were human or shifter and was not sure. He looked over at Aaron, who was having the same problem identifying them. Craig came to the front as well, leaving the girls protected between their cars and them.

Zach's eyes started to glow golden and the men took a step backwards, they seemed to be communicating between themselves although nothing could be heard. It looked like someone was talking to them and giving them direction.

"What do you want?" Zach asked.

"We heard there were some strangers in our area and wanted to know who it was and what you were doing?"

"If you had done your fucking homework you would have known there were strangers here already. Some of them have been living here for years," Zach said. Their eyes blackened the same as Abbey's and Jared's, reminding Katrina of the afternoon when she first found out her dear friends were shifters.

"Well we have just been told to come now, because you guys have popped up on our radar."

"What are you guys anyway? I can't smell you and cannot work out what you are!" Zach said.

"That's none of your business but you need to come with us. My boss wants to see you all."

"No fucking way are we coming anywhere with you," Aaron said as his and Craig's eyes changed to an eerie dark blue glow.

"You really do not want any trouble from us and you are asking for it," Craig said as he started to take his jacket off. Katrina was starting to shake nervously and Zach, feeling her mood change, stopped walking and pulled her closer into the protection of his body. She relaxed slightly when he bent down and kissed the top of her head.

"He just wants to find out who you are and what you're doing that's all."

"Okay, so why doesn't your boss show his ugly face, instead of sending all you goons?"

Just then there was movement in the back of the shadows and out walked a tall man in a grey suit.

He walked up to the man who had been trying to communicate with Zach and touched him on the shoulder. The new man stared at Zach's glowing eyes and then two his brothers' eyes. Zach started to read his mind.

The man in the suit was head of the crow shifters. They had been in Brisbane for over twenty years and they seemed to be the only ones there.

"So you are crow shifters and you're the boss. Ah!" said Zach.

"Actually the term is corvidae! You have quite a talent there, Mr ...?"

"Williams," Zach replied.

There was a hush and the brothers could see he was sending messages back through to his men. There were a couple of gasps and a few curses, as they must have worked out who the three brothers were.

The boss came forward and extended his hand as a gesture of goodwill. Zach walked over and shook his hand.

"I am sorry about that. I am Carl Sanchez, I run the flock here in the city so I make it my business to know if any new shifters move in to our territory. Anyone could be walking around here."

"Well, we won't be staying long, as we are only here to pick up our mates and take them home. One of whom has been living in this city for a long time," Zach said.

"I know about Abbey Hammond, if that's what you are implying? One of my men has kept a watchful eye on her over the years. He found Abbey and her eagle had always been very discreet about what she was and never caused us to worry," Carl said.

"I did not know you were in this area, I thought the royal family were still living in New South Wales?" said the guy that first confronted them.

"Well, we are not! Our family and close pack have just moved up into central Queensland. You might want to keep that in mind. My father will be very interested to know about you and your flock. How many members do you have?"

"We have fifteen in the group here, mainly the corvidae family and a couple of the accippitridae family. Our own families live away from the city for security reasons. There is also a family of six dromaiidae and a family of four dingoes," he heard Katrina say in his head. "What the -?" He turned around to her, amused, and said, "Crows, eagles and emus," then laughed.

"Great! Dingoes. I hate dingoes at the best of times," Craig said.

There was a giggle from the shadows which broke the ice. Carl and Zach exchanged phone numbers and introduced their groups so they could all meet each other.

"Is your father well?" Carl asked.

"Yes, he's good but needed to get away from the cold climate," Zach said.

"We have no issues with the royal family, or how long you want to stay. But you must understand we have kept this city free from trouble. It only takes one shifter to go off and change in front of a human and all hell breaks out."

"Have you heard of any werewolves in Queensland or New South Wales?"

"No. We don't normally mix well with were wolves, not that there are very many here in Australia. We

144

generally keep to our families but if you like, we can send out some inquiries on the crow network."

"Yes, that would be, good. Maybe with your help we might be able to track them. Thanks!"

"I will be in touch," said Carl and disappeared into the shadows he had come out of.

"Well, that was interesting, Abbey, have you ever come across Carl before?" asked Zach.

"No, but I think one of the guys stood back in the shadows looked familiar. I think I have seen him at the hospital. I think he's a porter," said Abbey.

"Okay. Well, it's getting late. I don't know about you guys but I am ready to call it a night. Please stay alert, family, we need to be watching out for anything suspicious and stay together we need to keep everyone safe. Somehow I don't think this trip is going to be easy," Zach said.

When they returned to the mansion and had driven through the security gates, Katrina asked Zach to take the small driveway around to the left, which led around to the back of the house. He looked at her questioning it and she flashed him a picture in her mind of all security lights coming on all over the outside of the house, the garden and huge spot lights in the trees.

Once inside her lounge, she walked over and flicked the switch down on the kettle to make them a drink. Zach lay down on the couch and noticed there was a flashing light from the internal phone system.

"You have a message?"

Katrina finished putting a couple of tea bags in their mugs and went to check it. It was from Rob.

"I am sorry, I got called away to the phone but I will be working late in my office tonight if you need to speak to me."

"Oh! Shit, I really didn't want to tell him that I needed to resign."

"I can come with you for support if you need it."

"No, I'll do it then it's off my chest. This whole thing is making me sick to the stomach."

She walked back into the kitchen and made his tea. He followed her to the bench and wrapped his hands around her tiny waist. She turned and nuzzled into his chest; she loved the way he smelled. He bent down and kissed her and she relaxed a little.

She let go of him and walked off to the front door. She turned and smiled and then was gone.

Katrina made her way to his office which was on the ground floor next to the dining room.

She knocked and waited for a response.

"Come in."

She walked in and found Robert sitting at his desk working on a couple of songs. He looked up and smiled at her. He really had the loveliest smile with dimples. She could see why the fans adored him. He was good looking with high cheek bones and blonde wavy hair parted down the centre. His eyes were the brightest blue that you could imagine floating in, reminding her of the sea.

She walked over to his desk and sat down in one of his leather seats.

"Come on, it cannot be that bad?" he said.

"I need to go home. My parents aren't coping without me. They have not stopped working since I left nearly two years ago and they are running themselves into the ground."

"I have only just seen this as I managed to get time off to go home. They have never mentioned anything to me, when I have spoken to them on the phone, because they knew I wanted a life in the city. I love the city and I love your children very much but I am so torn I don't know which way to go and if I could split myself in two I would."

He walked around the desk and gently pulled her out of her chair, holding her hands.

"If I could have a wish it would be that you stayed here with me, Martha and little Alex. I really do think of you as part of this family and I was really hoping that eventually you might even fall in love with me like you have with my children. You and my beautiful wife were the only ones who ever treated me like a real normal person, not a rock star, wanting to impress me all the time. It can be a very lonely life, not knowing who your real friends are and whether they really like you for yourself or they are just there for the rich lifestyle."

"I have to tell you this, you kind of got under my skin and I am wishing I should have said something now. But I can see the way you look at Zach and I know you would never look at me that way."

"I am sorry, I really had no idea. If I had, things might have been very different."

"It's all right. We will work it out together and I am sure you can always come back and visit us? Maybe we can all come to your home town and check it out. It would be nice for the children to keep in touch."

She hugged him and he hugged her back and kissed her on the cheek. He really did have feelings for her that she had no idea about. They stood for a while and then he broke away and went back to his desk.

"I will start advertising for a nanny tomorrow. There are a few agencies I will check out and we will need someone for the children and not because of your status. Will you want your mother to know?"

"Oh, shit. I forgot about her," he said.

Katrina was relieved that it was all over and that she was going home now. When she arrived back into the house Zach was still lying on the couch, dozing. She went over to him and sat down. He immediately jumped back when she sat down and his eyes started to glow. She looked at him and froze. He was hypnotising her with his power. He read the conversation that she had just had in Robert's office and the way he told her he cared for her. That he would give anything for her to stay and that he hoped she would fall in love with him. He saw the way they had embraced and he saw the way he was letting her go because of the way she loved Zach. He blinked and released her, but his griffin was still growling and very angry that there was another man's smell all over her.

"Stop all of this shit. This is ridiculous. Cut it out, the pair of you!" she yelled.

They both stopped and Zach's eyes changed back to normal and his griffin stopped growling.

"I am sick of all this shit you are putting me through. If I want to hug someone or give your brother some shit I am going to do it. Do I make myself clear?"

"We don't like our mate smelling of another male."

"I told you I would come home and that I will marry you next year. How much more do I need to do to prove it?"

"My griffin gets very jealous, he does not want to share you with anyone."

"Well, you had better be careful because Rob's behaving a lot better than you are right now. I can always change my mind and stay here! You know I can. It sure as hell would be a lot easier for those lovely children. That's for sure and there's no ring on my finger yet."

"Sorry. I mean it."

"I am warning you, if this happens again there will be consequences to pay. Got it?"

Zach nodded his head and picked her up to take her to bed. His griffin decided he needed to get rid of that smell once and for all!

Chapter 9

In the morning Katrina showered, trying to get some life back into her aching body. It was so much easier now without the plaster on her leg up. She decided to leave Zach sleeping in bed as he could always find her and hopefully he would be in a better mood than last night. She went downstairs to make a coffee before going over to the main house to find some breakfast. She was a little tired after the long day travelling, visiting the doctor in Townsville and then flying on to Brisbane. That would have been enough by itself without going out last night to the pizza restaurant. Meeting the crows, that was a scary confrontation and then the late meeting with Robert.

She sat and drank her coffee, thinking about it all. Not hearing Zach approach in just a pair of jeans.

"Are you all right, Kat? You look a little worried about something?"

She looked up and took in the picture of this man's physique. He was the most beautiful thing she had ever seen. In this body and his animal she really did love him, there was no question about it. She stood up and hugged him around the waist and kissed him on his lips. He wrapped his arms around her and just held her there, wanting nothing more than to feel her close to him. The internal phone buzzed and made them both jump. She walked over and picked it up.

"Hello?"

"Morning, Katrina dear. Are you coming over for breakfast this morning or do you need a tray?"

"No, we will be right there, just finishing a coffee."

"Okay!"

"That was Sheila, asking if we are coming over for breakfast? Do you need a shower first? I can make you a coffee once we over there."

"Give me five minutes." He ran upstairs and she could hear the watering running in the shower. She sat back down again and finished her coffee.

Katrina and Zach walked in to the kitchen to find Sheila busy cooking more bacon and eggs and Miles laying cutlery out on a silver tray. Katrina showed Zach where the coffee machine was and introduced Zach to Sheila. She smiled at him and her face went a little pink in colour.

"Can I help you with anything?" Kat asked Sheila.

"If you want to stick some bread in the toaster, we can all sit down and eat," Sheila said.

Zach sat down and watched Kat run around the kitchen making the coffees and the toast.

They all sat down to their breakfast and Katrina caught up with all the news from Miles and Sheila, of all the things that had happened while she been away.

Robert's mother had been constantly nagging at them to give the children more vegetables and fruit. She had also made a point of taking them out in the garden and the park at the back of the property to meet other children.

"Oh, great. So in just a little over five weeks she managed to break all Robert's rules about keeping them in a secure environment. Does she still take a security guard with her when she goes to the park?"

"Oh, no! She dismissed them when Robert was away, saying that Robert was wasting his money," Miles said.

"Yes, he's been trying to get them to come back ever since. It looks like they won't set foot in the place until she leaves. He said yesterday that he'd now employed another company and they will be starting in a few days," Sheila said.

"You have got to be kidding me, what a stupid – morning, Martha"

Martha came from nowhere, and jumped up onto Katrina's lap. She snuggled into her and whispered, "Granny's angry again."

"Oh dear, what did you do?"

"Nothing," she said, looking really sorry for herself, and went very quiet. Katrina finished her coffee and breakfast and then asked Martha what she wanted to do for the day. While she was waiting for an answer, Robert and his mother walked into the kitchen, with Robert swinging little Alex on his hip. Everyone started to get up until Robert told them all to sit back down and finish their breakfast. He apologised for disturbing their meal. His mother was carrying on like a stupid chook about something until she looked at Martha and asked her tell her Daddy what she had done.

"I tipped some stuff on the floor, Granny."

"Yes, that's right. But what was it, Martha?" said Mrs Saunders.

"I think it was smelly, it made my nose itchy," said Martha.

"Martha has just tipped my Chanel No. 5 all over the bathroom floor," cried out Robert's mother.

Zach looked at Katrina and sent her a telepathic message: "WTF?" She looked at him and sent back a response, "Fucking perfume, God knows how much it cost. It could be worth hundreds of dollars." He looked back and said, "Oh big deal."

"Yeah, to you maybe. I have never even smelt the stuff," Kat said.

"Well, now you can go into her bathroom," he said, looking away. She so wanted to laugh but was holding it in until Robert and his mother left the kitchen. As soon they were gone everyone burst out laughing. It was really hard not to under the circumstances.

"Does the cleaner come in today, Sheila?" Miles asked.

"Yes she will be in at nine o'clock. I suppose her ladyship's bathroom will be first on the list to be cleaned." Everyone laughed again.

The morning ran along smoothly with no more major perfume problems. Zach and Katrina spent most of their time upstairs in the nursery with the children. Zach was playing tea parties with Martha while Katrina was feeding Alex some milk. Through the morning Katrina had managed to ring up a couple of agencies and they were going to put together a list of desirable nannies. Katrina had instructed them what Robert would be looking for. They needed to be married or a widow and have a love for children. The nanny needed to live on the premises, so that might be an issue with a married person unless their partner could also acquire employment there. They needed to be responsible and caring and happy to travel abroad with Robert if needed. So with that in mind Katrina thought she would have hundreds apply.

Mrs Saunders came in and asked if they could take the children down into the garden to get some fresh air.

"That's a good idea. I can finish feeding Alex down there," Katrina said.

"Wonderful. Let's go, Martha. We can play on the swing set Daddy put in for you."

"Playing tea parties," Martha said.

"Well, Zach can come too!" Mrs Saunders said.

"No it's all right. I will make a few phone calls and do some more work on the cabins. I brought my laptop over," Zach said.

"We won't be long because it's nearly lunch time," Kat said.

Zach rang his father to let him know all the news since arriving in Brisbane. He told him about the crow shifters confronting them and the conversation Kat had had last night with Robert. When he had finished the conversation Katrina and the children were walking back in.

"Wow, that was quick!"

"Yes, it's too cold out there today. Maybe we can go out there tomorrow? Anyway, we are going to get ready for lunch and then these two little munchkins can have a nap."

"Do we get one too?" Zach said laughing.

"You can I am going to start on a job description for the next nanny. That should take a few hours."

"Okay, that's a good idea. I will get back to the website for the cabins." Zach sent Katrina a telepathic picture of the two of them kissing. She picked up a soft toy and threw it at him.

Over the next few days every one settled back into a routine. In the morning Zach and Katrina would go over and have breakfast with Sheila and Miles. Then the two of them would go to the nursery and spend the day with the children, Martha and Alex. When the children were ready for bed at night. Robert would come up and read to Martha and little Alex and stay there until they fell asleep, leaving Zach and Kat to spend the rest of the evening together in their little house eating dinner, watching movies, T.V. or reading.

Mrs Saunders had decided to fly home on Friday as she could see she was no longer needed. She wanted to help with the interviews for the new nanny but Robert had insisted she left the job to Katrina and himself.

On Thursday afternoon Katrina and Mrs Saunders took the children out into the garden to play on the swings. They both noticed a chauffeur-driven car pull up at the front of the house and some businessmen climb out. It was a normal event for Robert to have such meetings, so they carried on with what they were doing.

Martha had asked to go to the toilet and because Katrina was feeding the baby, Mrs Saunders suggested she would take Martha inside. When Robert's mother walked into the hall she heard a confrontation going on in Robert's office, with a lot of shouting. She picked up Martha and took her through to the toilet near the kitchen looking for Miles. There was still no sign of Miles in the kitchen and so she decided to go and look for him. She found him in the back garden with Sheila, helping her bring in the groceries from her car.

"Miles, there's a lot of shouting going on in the office and I am worried Robert might be in trouble," she called out to him. Miles and Sheila both looked at each other and hurried back into the kitchen dumping the groceries on the table. When they could hear things getting broken in the office Miles asked Sheila to ring the police. Mrs Saunders took off with Miles following a little behind her just as the men barged out through the office doors. At the same time Martha came running out of the toilet and Miles stopped to pick her up and run back to the kitchen.

"Sheila, please take Martha and keep her safe. We have trouble, run over and get Zach."

Zach had been working over at Katrina's house most of the afternoon, trying to sort out the website and speak to his father. He was talking to his father when he heard the yelling.

"Hey, there's something very wrong here. I'll ring you back."

"No! Zach, stay on the phone and tell what you see, I will get Amy to ring the boys now and send them over to you right away."

He did what he was told, his heart hammering in his chest. When he arrived at the kitchen he saw Sheila and Martha together, Sheila was talking to the police and ambulance service, giving them directions to the property on the telephone. She was holding back the tears and was shaking dramatically. He ran through to the main hall way, finding Mrs Saunders lying on the floor in a heap. He ran over and felt for a pulse in her neck but let out a growl when there wasn't one.

"Oh, fuck! Robert's mother is dead on the floor, looks like a broken neck. Where's Kat? Where the hell's Katrina?"

He then walked into the office and found Miles trying to save Robert. He had been very badly beaten up and he was trying to keep him breathing. He was relaying what he was seeing to his father.

"I am going to hang up, I need to search for my mate," he said just as Miles yelled, "They have taken her and the baby." Zach collapsed onto his knees where Robert and Miles were.

"Oh! God, no!" he yelled out.

His father roared down the phone. "I will get Craig to come back with the helicopter and pick me up then I will find these bastards and kill them. Get on to the crows and get them to help you until I get there."

Zach pressed the speed dial for his brothers, "We are on our way." Then he bent over to see if he could help Miles.

"What the hell happened?" Zach asked.

"The first thing I knew was that Robert' mother had come inside because Martha wanted to use the toilet. She walked past the office and heard yelling so she came and found me. I had just gone outside to help Sheila bring in the weekly groceries. When we got back to the office little Martha ran out of the toilet, so I picked her up and ran back to the kitchen. When I got back here they were heading off down the driveway with Katrina and Alex in the car. Poor Mrs Saunders was lying there in a heap and Robert in here, unconscious," Miles said, very distressed still trying to do CPR to Robert's chest.

"It happened so fast, almost too fast to be real," he said.

The ambulance screeched to halt at the front of the property and the paramedics came running into the hallway. Seconds later two police cars pulled up as well and four officers entered the hall. Zach went out to meet them while Miles stayed with Robert. It was chaotic for a while; the paramedics were trying to save Robert, who had been knocked unconscious with something hard. He was having trouble breathing and covered in blood.

They managed to find a sheet to put over Mrs Saunders until forensics came to take photos as little Martha was still in the house. The house was suddenly filled with at least twenty police officers, taking photos, asking questions and taping off the areas in the house that needed to be fingerprinted.

Zach was trying to hold it together but was slowly losing it. He was glad when he saw his brother enter through the front gates. Craig dropped Aaron off and then took off to the airport. When Aaron greeted Zach he pulled him into a bear hug and told him they would find her. Zach was too lost, he was a total mess and just shook his head. While they were huddled together he repeated what Miles had said about it all happening too fast. He asked Aaron to ring the crows and let them know what had happened. He then walked around the play area to see if there were any signs of what had happened.

All he found was the pram tipped over all the contents had been taken like his sheet and blanket. "Get photos of this, Aaron, and I will get the officers to come out and check for prints."

Two hours later Mrs Saunders's body had been moved and taken away by the forensic team. The ambulance had rushed Robert to hospital and he was on his way to theatre. Miles had identified one of the men that had come in as Maxwell Evans, Robert's old manager, the one he had sacked for not giving them enough gigs and working for the band. The manager that had been ringing him, causing him a lot of grief this last week and chasing him for lost money that he thought he deserved.

Martha stuck to Zach like sticky tape and kept asking where her Dad and Kat were. He had tried palming her off to Sheila but she would not have it. Martha just kept screaming at everyone until he picked her up.

Craig had left the airport and was on his way to Thistle Ridge. He would be back later that night with Richard.

Carl had called and was chasing down the plates with his friend in the police force. They wanted to find these men before the police found them.

Later that evening he got a faint picture in his mind of street signs going south. He sat up and looked at Aaron, and said very quietly, "They are going south. Katrina has just sent me a picture of Byron Bay."

There was a call from the main security gates and it was Carl. Miles let him through the gates and then walked to the front door to meet him. The crow shifter walked in, shook Zach, Aaron and Miles's hands and then walked around the front hall, going into Robert's office, trying to pick up any strange scents.

Zach asked Miles if he could take Martha back to the kitchen as she was now asleep. Sheila had dragged a small mattress from somewhere and made a bed up for her in the kitchen, as she refused to go to her own bed.

"I don't like what I am smelling here, something is very wrong!" Carl said

"What is it? We weren't able to smell anything. Like you guys, we couldn't smell you either," Zach said.

"That's because we use this spray most of the time that gets rid of our shifter smell."

"Well, that explains it. I thought this beak of mine was letting me down," Zach said.

"Well, it's not. They obviously know the secret of it too. The only problem is we can still smell it for some reason and it's dingoes."

"Your dingoes?" said Aaron.

"I don't know. I will ring them, but I can tell you this. If it is them, they won't live very long."

159

"My father is on his way and if he says those bastards will die they normally do," said Zach.

Carl dialled a couple of phone numbers but was getting nothing. The phones were turned off or out of range. He rang his second and asked him to go back through their files and find more phone numbers. Then he asked him to send someone around to their homes and check it out. He needed to know, even if it meant someone having to break in.

Aaron's phone rang and he walked away. Miles came back with some whiskeys on a silver tray and ushered them away from the office and hallway into the day room they had first been taken to when they all arrived. It was a comfortable room, with beige tones everywhere and cream walls. There were two loungers so they took one each. As Miles handed the whiskeys around, Zach asked if he had heard anything from the hospital.

"Hopefully tomorrow, we might have some better news," Miles said.

"Does Robert have any other siblings?" Zach asked.

"Not that I know of, I think it's only him and his mother. She lives over in Perth with a boyfriend and he lives here with the kids. I don't think he has any real girlfriends," Miles said.

"Well, I am sure the police will find out for sure," Carl said.

Aaron walked into the room and sat down.

"That was Craig. He is just refuelling and then will be on his way back with Dad. He is also bringing Jared with him."

"How did poor Jared get involved?"

"Well, when Abbey rang her family to let them know what had happened, he jumped up and down and said he

160

needed to come and help you. It's his sister after all, adopted or not. So the Hammonds have gone over to stay with Katrina's parents at the hotel until they find out more, leaving Andy to stay and keep an eye on everything at the farm."

"Oh, thank God for Abbey. I had forgotten about Kat's parents, I should have thought about them," Zach said.

"Mate, don't beat yourself up about it, you have been under a lot of pressure," Aaron said. "Why don't you try and have a rest for an hour or so? I will wake you if I hear anything."

"All right, but I will stay here in this room," Zach said, sliding his boots off, as he laid down on the lounger.

Miles disappeared and came back with some blankets and draped one over him.

"I'll be in the kitchen if you need me, sir!"

"Hey, Miles. Why don't you try and have a rest too?" Zach called out.

"I don't think I can close my eyes, sir. Every time I do I just see my master laying on the floor, all beaten up. Master Robert is going to be very shaken and upset when he finds out his mother's dead and Katrina and Alex are missing as well."

Aaron's phone beeped and it was Abbey.

"Still at the hospital nothing yet from theatre! Have you heard anything about Kat??" she texted.

"No! Nothing yet! Dad's on his way with Jared," Aaron texted.

"I might stay another hour and then come to you."

"Okay, Abs, see you soon."

"That's Abbey again. She stayed at the hospital after her shift finished tonight to see if she could help with

Robert. The nurses told her to go and have a rest and they would let her know, when they knew something. She says she had a sleep for a few hours and just woke up to find they are still in theatre," Aaron said.

"I am sorry to say it's not looking good," Carl said.

Chapter 10

Katrina was still travelling down the east coast of Australia and heading further and further away from home. The men abducting her and little Alex had not spoken a lot in the car, so she really had no idea where they were taking her or why. They had been driving nonstop since Brisbane, and she desperately needed to use the Ladies'. Trying to not to think about a rest stop, she tried to think of happier times as she was very scared and didn't want to provoke them.

She heard the chauffeur say something about being hungry and was relieved when she watched him pull in to a motel complex just off the high way at Coffs Harbour. One of the men sitting in the front of the car climbed out and went into the office and came back with some room keys. They all got out of the car, not saying anything to Katrina, so she stayed and sat there clutching Alex tightly to her.

"You can get out, girlie!" One of the men said and then another one of the men grabbed her by the arm and steered her roughly in the direction of one of the rooms.

"You can sleep in here for a few hours and then we are moving on again," he said.

"Is there anywhere I can find some nappies? I really need to change this baby and feed him?" Katrina asked.

"Go in to the room and I'll see what I can do," he said.

Katrina walked into the room and put Alex down on the carpet. It looked fairly clean and she really didn't have any other option. He had gone to sleep with the motion of the car travelling at a fast speed. But now having woken up after the car had stopped, he needed a drink and his nappy changed. Alex was getting a little whingey which did not help the situation. Katrina did not want him upsetting the men, they seemed nasty enough to do anything.

There was no way she was going to get any sleep unless she had a cot to put him into. Maybe they had one she could borrow, but then she didn't really want to ask the men for anything else. She turned on the television and tried to find a channel that might keep him amused while she went into the bathroom, locking the door.

When she came out, refreshed from a quick shower, there was a bag of groceries left at the bottom of one of the beds. Inside was a small packet of nappies, a baby's bottle and some fresh milk. She made up a bottle of milk straight away and gave it to Alex who sat back on one of the beds and drank it while she found a kettle and made herself a hot drink.

There was a knock at her door and when she opened it found one of the guards standing there. He handed her a warm, large paper bag, when she took it the smell was divine. When she peered inside there was a large packet of French fries and two hamburgers in it. She dug straight into the chips, not realising how hungry she was. She sat down and dug into the food, breaking up some of the other hamburger for Alex after it had cooled down. After she had eaten and fed Alex some of the hamburger she laid down on one of the beds. As she was watching Alex play on the floor with the takeaway cartons, she must have drifted off because the next thing she was aware of was Zach gently calling her name. She called back and was surprised when he answered her. Zach seemed to be trying to find her and wanted to know where she was.

When she realised that he wasn't with her, she told him she and Alex were in a hotel in Coffs Harbour. He then asked her if she was okay and she replied yes, but she was scared and very frightened and needed him.

"I need you too, my love," he said.

At daylight there was a tap on the door and someone calling out her name. She went to door to find a man standing there.

"You've got five minutes and then we are moving out."

"Okay," she said. Shutting the door, she made a quick stop to the bathroom, picked up the bag of baby items and a wriggling Alex. She was surprised to find that when she opened the front door the man was still there. Maybe someone had been outside her front door all night to make sure she didn't escape. He took the bag of groceries off her and walked with her to the car.

As she sat down and tried to put a seat belt on over her and Alex she noticed that the other men were standing outside the other room disagreeing about something.

"No! You don't know what you have done! I am afraid this really complicates things."

"Why the hell did you bring her? Why don't we just shoot her and the kid, be done with it? Or just leave them here, we could tie them up. The cleaner would eventually find them when she did the room services and by then we will have gone over the border."

"We are not killing, her you bloody idiot, you know who she's mixed up with? Carl Sanchez. He's one of the main gang leaders in Brisbane and friends with some very high up people. You kill her, and you may as well go and kill yourself."

There was still a lot of tension in the car when the chauffeur set off for their next part of the journey and nobody was saying anything.

They continued south again until the sign post for Raleigh came into view and they pulled into a service station. The chauffeur got out and started to fill up the tanks; another two men got out and walked into the service station to order food, leaving Katrina, Maxwell and the man they had called Ridgeway in the car. When Maxwell got out, saying he needed to go to the bathroom, Ridgeway turned to her and said, "We were just discussing what we are going to do with you! We had no idea you were connected to a group of shifters, and some of those shifters we have gained a lot of respect for, working with them over the years. This job has gone terribly wrong and Maxwell Evans has no idea what he's gotten us into."

"Does he know you are shifters?"

"No, he thinks we're just a group of bad ass blokes looking for a quick buck. Evans just employed us to beat your boss up a bit."

"Great! And you don't feel bad about that?" Katrina said.

"No. They are human, no offence."

"You do know they will try and find me?" Kat said.

"Oh yes! That's why we are getting further and further away. We need to get out of Queensland. Evans thinks it's his idea but after killing that woman who stupidly got in the way, we have no choice," Ridgeway said.

"You killed Mrs Saunders?"

She didn't know Mrs Saunders that well, but would never wish anything that bad on her.

"No, I didn't. Shorty did! He hates women of all kinds, shifters and humans. Unfortunately, she came in pushing her weight around at the wrong time. The rest you don't really need to know."

"Can I ask what sort of shifters you are?"

"Dingoes," he said with an evil grin. "Don't we look like dingoes?"

"No. I would have said bears, looking at the size of you all. But then there are none in this country, are there?"

Katrina felt a big knot in her stomach and thought she was going to throw up. How could these people be so cold? Looking around whilst sitting in the car she noticed a car and caravan pull in to the service station. When the door of the car opened and the driver jumped out she could not believe her eyes, it was the man from the hotel. Mr Donohue and his wife said they were heading back to Melbourne and had even offered to give her a lift back to Brisbane. She watched the wife go into the shop and turned around and asked Ridgeway if she could go to the bathroom.

What she did not expect was that Ridgeway got out of the car and walked with her to the bathroom. She needed to think quickly what to do. Standing outside the ladies', Kat asked Ridgeway if he could hold the baby while she went in.

As she was coming out of one of the stalls, Mrs Donohue was coming in to the toilets. Her eyes lit up when she saw Katrina but Katrina quickly put her fingers up to her mouth to silence Mrs Donohue.

Mrs Donohue sniffed the air and suddenly went pale as she mouthed, "Dingoes," and Katrina nodded. She pulled a pen out of her purse and pulled a hand towel down from the wall and gave it to Katrina who wrote as fast as she could:

"Kidnapped by men (dingoes). Please contact Dad, who will contact the royal family. Have killed my boss's mum! I don't know how anyone else is."

She passed it to Mrs Donohue, squeezed her hand and walked out. Ridgeway escorted her back to the car and then they were on their way again.

The driver slowed down just outside Raleigh and took a turn off the Pacific Highway and onto B78 they started heading towards the town of Fernmount. Katrina acted like nothing had happened and tried to feed Alex some hot chips. She had to bite the sharp edges off and blow on them. Why the hell didn't they just bring her a sandwich for the baby? It was breakfast after all.

Dumb arse! she thought.

They carried on for another hour and a half until they reached the small town of Bellingen, where they stopped, and pulled into the car park of a supermarket to pick up food and supplies. Katrina was allowed to get out of the car and stretch her legs, but Ridgeway watched her carefully, making sure she was not going to call out to anyone or try and run.

Another twenty minutes later they were back in the car with a heap of groceries and heading down a road called Bowraville which was on the outskirts of Gladstone State Forest. At the end of a dirt road they stopped at a property surrounded by tee trees and scrub.

They all climbed out and without speaking to each other, started to do different tasks. The chauffeur unpacked the car, while one collected some firewood from around the yard and lit the fire inside. Another one went straight out to the back of the property and was checking around the back perimeter. Once they were done Ridgeway escorted Katrina inside the house. He led her to a small bedroom where she was asked to stay. She was given the baby's things and then locked inside.

She put Alex down on the floor and looked around. There was a tiny window behind her that a child could possible get through but she didn't think she would fit. Two narrow single beds with dusty pink blankets on and a little lamp that needed oil. *This place had not been lived in for years,* she thought.

The other window she could look out of was barred with pieces of timber.

She sat down on one of the beds and watched the dust rise around her. Thinking of Zach, she pulled out her necklace that had been stowed away under her tee shirt and rubbed it. Seeing the beautiful necklace, she suddenly thought of home and her family and Zach the tears started to roll down her face until she had a lump in her throat and slowly started to cry.

It was just daylight when Carl woke up, hearing a beeping but was unsure where it was coming from. He walked outside in the hall to see Aaron talking on the phone, and to find the sound had disappeared. He walked back into the lounge to find it was in there and as he walked closer towards Zach it was getting louder. Carl stood over him, wondering what it was as he called out to Aaron. Aaron came into the room and joined Carl, who was just standing over Zach staring. As if on cue Zach suddenly woke up.

"Guys you really know how to freak someone out! Do you want to give a heart attack?"

"Mate, you are seriously beeping."

"Ah!"

"Mate, you are seriously beeping. No bullshit!" Aaron said.

"What? Oh, shit. It's Katrina's necklace, she must have activated it."

"Brother, you are not making any freaking sense."

"After the last time I swore it would never happen again. You remember when Katrina's phone didn't work giving us a GPS reading, directing to us to where she and the horse were after getting bitten by that bloody taipan? Well I decided to get a necklace made with all the diamonds and gemstones that the girls love. But I also had a sensor transmitter put in to the back of the pendant. Which of course she would never know was there unless at some stage she needed help like now and activated it."

"And how did she suddenly activate it?" asked Carl.

"It might seem strange but it works on a stress level, something must have really upset her. Her blood pressure is up or she's crying and breaking down."

"Okay. So how do you find out where she is?" asked Aaron

"Well, her necklace should give me a reading which was set up on a program installed on my laptop."

"All right, let's go!" Aaron said. Carl's phone rang and it was his second wanting to talk to him. He waved to them and then walked outside into the garden leaving them in the hall. Just then Zach's phone buzzed.

"Hello!"

"Zach it's me, we have just arrived at the airport. We are going to refuel and then jump into the car and come over to you," Richard said.

"Okay, Dad, Craig knows how to get here. Katrina has set off her transmitter; we are just going to track it. I should have a reading by the time you get here. The last time I made contact with her, the dingoes had pulled up at a motel near Coffs Harbour."

"We have the police alerted here and in New South Wales, they should all be out looking for the car. They know it's a murder investigation and a kidnapping."

Zach and Aaron took off through the house to get to the apartments at the back. They took a short cut through the kitchen to find Miles and Sheila still sleeping. Sheila had moved on to the made-up bed and was snuggled up tight to Martha, nice and warm by the Ray-Burn.

Miles being a light sleeper opened his eyes and jumped.

"It's all right, Miles, we are just going through to Katrina's lounge. I am going to get a few things and pack some clothes for us both. Craig and my father are on their way here from the airport, they should be arriving soon. Would you mind opening the gates? We might be heading off in a while and could really do with some coffee."

"No problem, sir. I'll get right on it. Maybe some breakfast too?"

"That would be awesome, Miles, I am starving. Can we make it to go?" said Aaron.

"No problem, I'll have it made soon."

Zach took off up the stairs and threw some clothes in a bag for him and Katrina. He came down and opened his computer up to the transmitter program. Once he processed a few commands it started to generate a map of Queensland. As they watched the map, an arrow moved down the coast to Raleigh and there it started to flash.

"You beauty!" Zach said.

"Holy fuck! Come on! If that's where she is, let's go? Why are we waiting around?" asked Aaron.

"Aaron, if we go racing in there, they will kill her for sure and little Alex. We have to seriously think about this," Zach said.

"I just wish I could do something."

"Hell! We all do! But Dad will say the same thing," Zach said.

They walked back to the kitchen and found Miles, Sheila, and little Martha cooking breakfast. Martha ran into Zach's legs as soon as she saw him, he bent down and picked her up. She snuggled up to him like she had known him for years. He found it quite strange, as normally he seemed to frighten children, but not her. After Miles informed them that his other brother had returned with his father they walked back through the house to the day room.

"Father, it's good to see you, and how good of you to come!" Zach said shaking his hand, still holding Martha. His father pulled him into a quick hug and said. "Nonsense, Katrina is family. I need to be here."

Zach saw Jared standing on his own and walked over to meet him, they shook hands.

"Thanks for coming as well to help me, it means a lot, Jared."

"Hey, no problem, she's my sister. I need to help find her and bring her home. Then hopefully you can keep her at home this time."

"I am certainly planning to do that with your help, Jared. When we get back to Twin Hills I am banning her from going anywhere, even out in the garden, without me. It looks like even being out in a freaking garden is not secure enough for my mate."

"So what is the news?" Richard asked

"Okay, well we have located her in Raleigh, south of Coffs Harbour and looking at the map, it seems like they are a little way inland of that town. When we looked before on the computer screen it looks like there's several national parks around that area so maybe they have pulled up in a camping area or a dwelling or something. But the transmitter has stopped in that one area and has not moved again!" Zach said.

Miles walked in with mugs of coffee and bacon and egg rolls. Everyone sat down and dug in. Zach's phone buzzed and it was Charlie.

"Charlie, is everything alright? I am sorry I didn't contact you myself. I have been under a little stress, which you would understand."

"Yes! It's fine, Zach, we were just waiting for news about Katrina?"

"I am sorry, Charlie, we have no word yet. Father is here and we are making a plan now. We are going to leave here soon and follow the kidnappers down the coast. The police force has been out there searching and it seems they are somewhere near Raleigh."

"Yes, I know, Zach. I have just had some news, that's why I contacted you. Mr Donohue has just rung me; remember the guy you were querying about at the hotel. Well, he just rang to let me know that his wife bumped into Katrina at the service station in Raleigh when she walked into the toilet. Katrina passed a message to her and it said: 'Been kidnapped by dingoes, four of them and ex manager Evans who has no idea about them, still heading south to get out of Queensland because of killing Robert's mum. They seem to think if they get over the border that the New South Wales police will be more lenient. Not," Charlie said.

"Thanks, Charlie, that's awesome. We are really going to have to thank Mr and Mrs Donohue," Zach said.

"I really thought there was something funny going on, son. I mean I don't know why Katrina is calling the men dingoes. Maybe a code or something, but Mr Donohue followed the abductors' car along the highway for several hours and watched them turn off the main highway and onto the B78 by pass heading towards Gladstone State Forest. The Donohues kept following them until they turned down a private dirt road and could no longer follow."

"That's great, Charlie, thank you so much. Can you let them know we will be there as soon as possible and thank them for helping us?"

"Okay, I will ring them back now. Mr Donohue also said he would wait around for you just in case you needed any help."

"Well, if they are still there, when we arrive I will thank them myself."

"See you later and bring her home, Zach," Charlie said.

"I will Charlie and next time she gets the shits with us all, I will lock her up in one of the cabins."

"Yes, please, Zach. We never want this to ever happen again!" Charlie said.

They both hung up and Zach said, "Okay. Well, the couple, Mr and Mrs Donohue who were staying at the hotel and who we thought were suspicious because they were over friendly to Katrina. Anyway, they bumped into Katrina at a service station in Raleigh. Katrina managed to pass on a message to Mrs Donohue in the ladies' toilet saying that she was with dingoes and the ex-manager, and that they were heading out of Queensland. She was aware that Mrs Saunders has been killed; one of them told her that. The Donohues waited for them to leave and then followed Katrina's kidnappers to find out which route they had taken. They have also kept watch on them, and know where they turned off on the highway and the private land they have gone to."

"Wow! Even I feel guilty, brother," said Craig.

"Invite them to your wedding!" said Aaron.

"Wedding," said Martha.

Everyone looked at this small child, forgetting that she had been there the whole time.

"Okay, people, let's focus. We need to get down there as soon as possible. The helicopter is fuelled and ready to go. We can travel with five people but we will need to bring back Katrina and the baby," Richard said.

"I am going to leave and see if I can chase up some crows in that area. I have a cousin down there who might be able to help with something. I'll ring around when I get back to the office and then I'll contact you later," Carl said.

"Thanks, Carl, we probably won't need the help but it is always good to have backup," Richard said.

"I will stay here with Miles and keep an eye on the place. We are going to need to keep the place locked up and away from the TV cameras and journalists that will be swarming around today. If this story has already hit today's morning news all the TV channels will be all trying to get in here. Asking questions and trying to get pictures for a story. Hopefully the security guards will arrive today," Aaron said.

"Aaron, you ring us if you hear anything at all!" Richard yelled as he walked out of the door, followed by Jared and Craig.

"Yes! I will."

Zach took off to the kitchen and put Martha down next to Sheila, who was making some fruit cakes.

"I am going to have to leave you with Sheila, Martha. I have to go and find your brother and Katrina. I will be back later, and hopefully have Alex with me," Zach said.

"Can I help cook with Sheila?"

"Yes you can help me make some patty cakes and we can put some smiley faces on them," Sheila said.

Zach gave Martha another cuddle before walking out and jumping into the back of the car with Jared.

Thirty minutes later they were back at the airport, sitting in the helicopter waiting for Craig to do his flight checks and get clearance from the tower to leave.

Jared had been checking the areas around Raleigh for a landing strip or somewhere large enough to land a helicopter. They didn't want to let the kidnappers know they were coming and needed to creep up on them without being seen.

Zach sat in the back next to him, not really listening to all their conversations. He was deep in thought, worrying about Katrina, dreading that they might have already hurt her, or worse, they had plans to kill her and the baby. Every time he thought of that it made him sick to the stomach. He really didn't know what he would do if he lost his love, and it was really cutting him up. He would find it hard to live without her and was trying not to think about that right now. She was so much a part of him now they were truly united; she was his life.

The helicopter took off and followed the coastline down to the Gold Coast and several hours later, on to Raleigh. Once they arrived, they followed the traffic along the highway until they found the turn-off for the Gladstone State Forest.

"According to this map, we should be able to put down in an old airstrip at Bellingen. It's only got a short run way built for the flying doctors, using a Cessna Grand Caravan. But it's big enough for us as we don't need a runway, just the space for the helicopter to land," Jared said.

"Good work! I think we should fly over the property but keep going so they don't suspect anything, and then come we will come back on foot," Richard said.

Craig suddenly came over the internal radio, telling them all through their headsets that they were approaching a property on the left-hand side of the helicopter. They all looked out and spotted an old-looking shack, with a large black Cadillac outside the front of the building. They flew over it and noticed there were a few men out the front sitting on the veranda and a couple outside the back of the property.

"Okay! Let's fly past so they don't get suspicious," Richard said to Craig.

They flew on further until they were right out of range of anyone seeing and then they doubled back to the town of Bellingen. Once they found their way to the airfield they landed and made their way back on foot.

As they were walking across the main street Zach's hair started to rise on the back of his neck. His father turned around and looked straight at him as though he felt it too. They stopped and looked around the street for any signs of danger. There were a couple of children playing outside the bakery, one pushing the other on a tricycle. On the other side of the road, there was an old lady in a long red coat wheeling a shopping trolley, to her car. Just as they were watching her they noticed a guy coming out of the pub, carrying a carton of beer. Zach's sensors were warning him that this was the guy, so they pretended they were doing something else. Zach walked back across the road and pretended he was going in the pub, to see where the guy was going.

He watched as the guy walked back around the corner and in to the side alley, where there was the same black Cadillac. Zach could not believe his luck and signalled for the others to come.

The side alley was empty apart from the man carrying his carton of beer, so it was easy for Zach to run up behind him and tackle the man to the ground. He dropped the carton and was about to start swinging his fists, when Zach made eye contact and turned the guy into a hypnotised zombie. By the time the rest of them came around the corner Zach was interrogating the man.

"Who are you and what have you done with Katrina?" asked Zach.

"She's at the house being guarded by Shorty and Ridgeway."

"Has she been harmed at all?"

"No. Evans told us to bring her in the car, with the baby, so that we could blackmail Saunders for some more money. But when Shorty grabbed her and threw her in the car we could all smell eagle shifter on her. We didn't know what to do with her. Evans doesn't know any of this. It's a big mistake and now we are trying to get further away from Queensland and hide from the people that will be looking for her," The man said, still zoned out.

"Oh, dear! You mean us! I think your day has suddenly got worse," Richard said.

"You can now show us where you have been hiding out. I am sure Craig would not mind driving this nice car," Zach said.

"I am hoping for your sake that nobody has hurt my daughter, otherwise I am afraid you will all end up dead," Richard said.

"I am hoping that too! I feel like hurting someone today," Jared said.

They all climbed in the car, Zach keeping eye contact with the kidnapper. Zach read his mind and tried to blank off the internal messages coming from his pack. They were wondering where he was and what was taking so long. Zach managed to interfere with his brain, sending back a message to say he was coming.

By the time they got back to the shack, the sun was going down. They stopped a little way back to let Richard and Jared out of the car. They automatically shifted and instead of two men standing by the car, suddenly there was a large eagle and a huge lion.

They pulled up at the front door in the Cadillac and all climbed out. Ridgeway was coming back from the tree line and started to howl. Evans came running from around the back of the house with a loaded gun, aimed at whoever was the problem. The other two muscles came walking out of the house, and then they all stood surveying the danger.

"What do you want?" Evans asked.

"We want Katrina and the baby, that's what we want," Zach said

"What makes you think we have them?" Ridgeway asked.

"We have had people following you since you left Brisbane and you are the only ones driving a black Cadillac. The police have been following you as well, this is now a murder investigation and a kidnapping," Craig said.

"You have no right to come here, making your demands. Can't you see I have a gun, and these guys are not going to let you take what's mine!" Evans said.

"She's not yours! She belongs with me; she is my mate. Do you guys all feel the same way?" Zach asked looking around at the men.

"You are outnumbered, mate, and I don't see you getting anywhere near her!" Ridgeway said, laughing.

"I was so hoping you would say that, dingo!" Zach said as he and Craig changed.

Suddenly there was a huge griffin on the ground beside a wedge-tailed eagle. The men looked around at each other and you could tell by their expressions they had definitely made the wrong choice. Without any warning the kidnappers changed into dingoes and started to gallop to towards the griffin and the eagle. Out of the bush came a roaring lion and another eagle, white and grey in colour. A couple of minutes later they were followed two large black wolves. The wolves went straight in for the kill, taking out one of the dingoes. Zach launched himself at the manager trying to make a break for it. Evans tried to aim the gun at Zach but was he shaking too much, he pulled the trigger and missed Zach, hitting the trees behind him. Zach picked him up like he weighed nothing and threw him back against the tree trunk, snapping his neck. He then ran into the shack, looking for Kat and the baby, while Richard picked up another dingo and threw him against the ground. As he was running he could hear limbs getting snapped. Zach sent out his griffin sensors and could feel his mate. She seemed to be in the last room down a narrow hall way and the door was bolted from the outside. He smashed through the door and there she was, holding Alex tight to her chest, sitting on the floor near the tiny window. She was shaking very badly and crying, she put little Alex down and walked over to Zach. She hugged him around his large neck and sobbed hard, she had never been so happy to see him. He shimmered back into his own body and was surprised to see little Alex smiling up at him. He had not been frightened by the strange creature at all and sat back clapping his hands together. Zach held Katrina for what seemed like an hour but was only a few minutes. Then he picked up Alex and took Katrina by the hand and walked out through the front door of the shack. They were met by two wolves, two eagles and a large lion roaring and four dead dingoes, still in the dingo form; and a dead manager.

As soon as they saw Katrina and Alex they all started to shift back into their human form.

Richard was the first to come over and hug Katrina, followed by Jared and Craig. Mr and Mrs Donohue stood there and waited until the family had finished hugging each other before coming over to join in. Richard shook their hands and welcomed them into the family, introducing them to everyone.

"We are so glad we managed to help you. I was so frantic when I saw Katrina at the service station with those bastards. I wanted to kill them all then, but it was day light and there were too many people around," Mrs Donohue said.

"We really hate dingoes because they cause problems where ever they go. Carrie and I have had problems with a small group in Melbourne. They seem to think they are better than the rest of us," Mr Donohue said.

"I would really like to thank you both for your help. I really appreciate what you have done, I am really sorry for being suspicious at the hotel, but I thought you were trying to kidnap my mate. We had just moved into the area and we were still on our guard trying to protect a new territory. Next time you come up to Queensland, maybe you would be our guests?" Zach said.

Katrina walked over and hugged Mrs Donohue and then her husband.

"By next year we will have the Black Boulders Resort ready for the tourist season. So please come and visit us. We would really be honoured," Katrina said.

"That would be wonderful, I am sure we can do that. We might even look at real estate while we are up there too. We keep saying that we will move further up the coast line to be nearer our daughter. Don't we, Carrie?"

"That sounds good, to me! Any way time is going on. We might get out of here and let you sort out what you are going to do with this situation," Mrs Donohue said.

They all said their goodbyes and watched as the Donohues walk off down the dirt lane.

"Okay, I will call the police after I speak to Toby, my shifter friend in the police force. The story will be that we got here after following the manager's Cadillac from town, after we had a tip-off that the car had been spotted in this area. But by the time we arrived on foot, the men must have taken off in another car, as the place was deserted except for Alex and Katrina," Richard said.

"What about the body and dead dingoes?" Jared asked.

"They will think that the men had a fight, amongst themselves and the manager pulled a gun on one of them. Or maybe he threatened all of them, making them leave. Which is true, the police can find the bullet in the tree over there. The dingoes are another problem, maybe the men had a pack of dingoes bothering them last night.

You know howling and carrying on, because they themselves were shape shifter dingoes and the kidnappers decided to kill them?" Zach said.

"How do humans kill dingoes? Won't that look a little weird?" Jared asked.

"Yes that's true. Are there any other guns? Maybe we need to hide the dingoes?" Craig said.

"Okay! Let's look for another gun, and then if there is one I want each dingo shot. If there is only the Evans gun then we will hide the dingoes in the shrub, somewhere where they won't be seen. Then after the police have finished here we will burn them and get rid of any trace of them," Richard said.

Half an hour later the police arrived on the scene. It was very dark but with car lights they saw Evans's broken body next to the tree where he had landed. They found the gun and bagged it for finger prints and after a while one of them found the bullet in the tree. Luckily for the dingoes, they were hidden in the scrub and no one knew any different. As it was dark no one seemed to notice the blood on the grass, from the dingoes. The body was taken away by the forensic that had flown in from Raleigh and they were going back to the local hospital to do a post mortem.

After getting statements from Richard and Zach they were able to leave and head back to Brisbane. Even though they were going over state lines, as they were now in New South Wales, but between Richard and Zach they had helped change the police officers' minds.

And so the police officers went away two hours later, happy that they had found the body of a murderer. The police were now blaming Evans for Mrs Saunders's death and also for organising the kidnapping and mystery disappearance of Katrina and Alex. For their reports, they would certainly look good for the TV crew, which had somehow found their way into Bellingen.

No more was said about the rest of the kidnappers and the Williams family were given lifts back to the airport. There was a camera crew which it seemed had been tipped off by someone and were waiting for them when they arrived. Richard ushered Katrina and the baby into the back seat whilst Craig and Zach took the front seats. They still had to wait for Jared who was getting rid of the dingoes. He had stayed in eagle form and carried the dingoes away, to different areas. No one would really notice one or two dead dingoes; most farmers baited them as they were always a nuisance, killing stock.

Jared arrived fifteen minutes later in human form, running up to the helicopter. He climbed into the back with Katrina and Richard and Craig took off. Once they were in the sky, Richard asked Jared how he went. He told them across the internal radio that he had separated them and left them in high scrub where no one would ever find them. Zach texted Aaron again and let him know they were on their way back and to let Miles know they would all be glad of a bed for the night. They really needed to stay together and no one was going to let Kat out of their sight. Alex was asleep when they landed and there was another camera crew waiting by the arrivals. They were so glad when they found two police cars waiting for them where they had been asked to land. Once they parked Katrina was ushered again by Richard and Zach to the waiting police car. They all climbed in and moved straight towards the highway heading to Roberts home. The second police car waited for Craig and Jared whilst they closed up the helicopter.

It was very late when they arrived at the Saunders mansion, everyone was weary and in need of showers.

There were security guards on the front gates letting them in. Miles stood by the front doors to welcome them home when they walked in.

Katrina was hugged for about ten minutes by the Saunders staff, Aaron and Abbey. She really needed some sleep but could not relax yet. Abbey took Alex off of Katrina and carried him up to bed with Sheila. They planned between them to feed him and bath him before bed. Miles poured everyone a whiskey in the lounge as they all tried to relax and talk about what had happened.

As Katrina's eyes were shutting, Zach excused them and carried her to bed. Once she arrived upstairs in her lovely bedroom she asked Zach to help her undress from the clothes she had been wearing to wash away any sign of the dingoes. He and his griffin agreed and walked into the bathroom to turn on the shower. He gently helped her out of her dirty torn clothes and carried her to the shower. He quickly stripped and joined her in the shower, where he held her under the hot water. She let the water run over her tied body as he washed her back and shoulders. Zach then washed her hair with some sweet smelling shampoo. She finished rinsing herself while waiting for Zach to finish washing himself. He wrapped her in a thick towel after they had finished and then carried her back to bed. He slowly dried her all over and then lifted her into bed under the blankets. He followed her soon after and they snuggled up close together, in the foetal position.

Zach and his griffin wanted her so badly, they needed to claim her again but she was exhausted. They would have to wait until tomorrow and then he could really work on getting rid of that smell. There was no way he was going to let his mate smell like that for long.

She dozed off to sleep and before long was quietly snoring, he held her close to his chest until he too dropped off to sleep several hours later.

Chapter 11

Katrina stirred early in the morning, wondering where she was and nearly jumped out of her skin when she found she was naked. With her heart racing hard against her chest she looked down feeling an arm around her waist. But soon relaxed when she turned and realised it was Zach sleeping beside her.

Katrina laid back down again, relieved to find she was safe, and was surprised when Zach's hand came up from around her waist and started stroking her body, lightly with his fingertips. He obviously was awake and doing a great job making her breasts grow hard and her nipples stand up tight. From the feel of his strong fingers feather touching her skin. She was tingling from the sensations he was sending down through her spine. Her whole body was alive with an electric current making her heart increase its beating. Zach pushed up closer to her and she could feel his hard length sticking into her back. He explored, moving his fingers around in circles until he reached between her thighs and was excited when he found wetness, between her slick folds. She was so ready for him, and in a fast motion he turned her onto her hands and knees and spread her legs apart until he was able to inline his thick penis into her entry. She gasped at the pleasure of him entering and filling her completely and held on to the pillows for support, still wondering how that happened so fast.

He held her around the waist whilst he thrust in and out of her, trying to leave nothing between them but air.

He really needed to get as far into her channel as possible, leaving his scent there, claiming her again, and his griffin wanted it too. Zach continued kissing and caressing her neck and shoulder whilst pumping further and further into her. When Zach touched her between the folds and squeezed her clitoris between his fingertips roughly, Katrina took several deep breaths and exploded into a huge orgasm, leaving her body shaking all over.

Her whole body had gone to jelly and her legs and knees could longer hold her up.

Zach supported her again around the waist with both hands holding her up before pumping as hard as he could several times before he climaxed, shooting his seed deep inside her. She was still coming down from her climax several minutes later when they both collapsed on to the bed. Zach kissed her on the lips and she snuggled back against his hard chest. That's where they stayed until there was a knock at the door.

Zach climbed out of bed, grabbing his boxers and went down stairs to see who it was. He opened the door was met by his father, whose face was full of worry.

"Morning, Father. Is everything alright?"

"Sorry, son but, no it's not! The police have just called around and let us know that Robert passed away last night. They think he had a blood clot in his brain and never regained consciousness."

"Abbey never said anything last night when we got here so I thought he must have pulled through. Shit, after the entire nightmare we went through yesterday I did not really think about him. I suppose that's bad," Zach said.

"No it's not, she didn't know. Abbey stayed there after her shift, but when she hadn't heard anything after six hours she came here to see what was happening with Katrina. The nurses never got back to her," Richard said.

"So what the hell do we do now?" Zach asked.

"Well it looks like we are going to be here a week or two more until we find out what's going to happen with the children. I know we won't be able to take Katrina home while this is all going on."

"She will be devastated. Robert had confessed his love for her and he was hoping she would marry him. He could see how she loved his children and was hoping for the same. But he never said anything until I arrived back here with her. He had said Kat was the only one that took him for what he was. A widowed father of two children and not some glamorous rock star, that women drooled all over and try to get in his bed for quick shag," Zach said

Katrina came down the stairs with her hair still wet from the shower. They both looked up at her and she knew something was wrong.

"Honey, the police have been over this morning and have given us some bad news. I am afraid Robert passed away last night. They seem to think he came through the surgery but later had a blood clot to his brain," Richard said carefully.

"Oh! God, can this get any worse? What are we going to tell the children? Who is going to take them? Oh God! This can't be happening," she cried. Zach walked up to her and encircled her into his strong arms for a hug. She stayed there crying for a while and then looked up at them both and said.

"We will need to take the children back with us to Twin Hills, that's the only safe solution."

"Okay, Kat, we will look at that later, but for now let's go and see where these kids are," Zach said.

"I'll go and help Sheila and Miles while you have a quick shower. Then we can discuss who should tell

189

them, and maybe chase down any relatives?" Katrina said, as she walked out of the front door leaving Zach and his father in the lounge.

"I would like to find out a little more about Robert's wife, how she died, and her background. Her parents, where she came from. You know that sort of thing. Something happened yesterday and I have a feeling someone is hiding secrets," Zach said.

"All right, we will get onto it. I have a feeling your mate is not going to let go of these kids without a fight," Richard said.

"Well, if my sensors are working correctly, I don't think it will come to that," Zach said.

Zach climbed the stairs two at a time and headed for a shower. When he came down ten minutes later the place was empty. He made his way over to the kitchen and found everyone in there.

Abbey and Aaron were stuck at the hip, embracing and talking quietly in the corner. Sheila and Miles were busy cooking bacon and eggs for breakfast and Katrina and Richard each had one of the children on their laps and were feeding them. Zach thought that the only thing wrong with this picture was that they were in Brisbane and not at Thistle Ridge. Things would not need to change that much, if his plan went the right way. Miles and Sheila may not want to continue to stay with the children but he was hoping that they would.

After breakfast the children were taken up to the nursery where Abbey and Katrina played dress-up with Martha while Alex had his little morning sleep. Richard and Zach asked Miles if they could find out more about the children's mother and Miles pulled out everything from files that he could find. They found photos of Robert, Martha and his wife before they had Alex and there were documents of births, for Robert and Martha. There was a death certificate for Louisa and a marriage certificate between Robert and Louisa Grant. But no birth certificate for Louisa Grant, it was like she didn't have one or she didn't want it found. They spent most of the day in Robert's office but could not find it. After a while Zach went and checked on the girls. He wanted to see his mate and make sure she was where she was supposed to be.

"Hello, stranger. Long time no see. We are just going to put on *Toy Story* for the second time, if you want to join us?" Katrina asked.

"Well, I would love to, but I am really on a mission," he said, smiling at her.

"Can I help you with something?" she asked.

"What a stupid question, Kat. Of course you can help him with something! Der!" said Abbey, raising her eyebrows and shaking her head. They both laughed and then he turned to Kat and asked; "Do you know if Louisa, Martha's mother, had a place of her own in this house? We are trying to find some paperwork and are not having any luck?"

Katrina looked across to Martha and said, "Sweetie, did Mummy have a special place where she went in the house? That was really her own and nobody else went there? Like a secret?"

Martha looked at her and then back to Zach, she held out a hand to Zach and led him away.

They walked along the hallway on the second floor, past several rooms until they reached the stairs going up to the third floor. The staircase was another bold spectacle of red carpet and polished timber balustrades. Designed by a craftsman, and yet the third floor was very rarely used, and such a waste.

Zach, still holding on to Martha's hand and struggling to keep up with her little strides, decided to pick her up and run up the remaining steps.

Katrina had followed closely behind, watching Martha carefully and letting her show Zach where Mummy's hiding spot could be found. Little Martha had really taken a shine to her mate, and he to her. She really loved the two of them dearly. It was funny to see Zach acting so paternal; maybe he had more family she hadn't met. Even Abbey had taken on the role of looking after the baby, *maybe shifters have parental instincts built into them,* she thought.

When Martha reached the last room on the right-hand side, they were met by the late afternoon sun shining from under the door. As they walked in they found a sun room. It was warm and decorated in lovely soft yellow tones. Beside the huge window was a rocking chair with lemon cushions and beside it a small nest of tables. Looking around they noticed the décor was fresh and modern with the timber furniture being all white washed and then scuffed with a sander to give it that rustic feel.

"This was definitely Louisa's room," Katrina said to Zach.

They decided that this was what Martha had come to show them as there did not seem to be anything that looked like a hiding spot to them, until Martha walked over to a large wardrobe, opened the door and climbed through it. They looked at each other and then both rushed to the wardrobe to see her disappear towards some narrow stairs. Martha started to climb again, taking them higher and higher, up to the attic. Up on the last step they found a small door painted blue, they stood back and watched Martha open it and walk in. It led them into a small office, with skylights in the roof. The desk was full of paper work and journals, covered in leather bindings.

"Do you think this was Louisa's home?" Kat asked Zach.

Zach turned around and looked at Katrina and said, without talking; "It could have been. We need to get Martha out of here so we can go through all this paperwork. I don't want her getting upset if we are rooting through her mother's special room. But I feel there are answers here and we need to check it out."

The journals they picked up dated from the present day back to 1765. Each journal had the same handwriting, and no mistaking it. It was Louisa's. Zach pulled out his phone and texted his father.

"Hey, Dad! I think you need to see this, we are on the third floor, last room on the right and then climb through the wardrobe to the attic."

"Okay, we are coming," Richard texted back.

Katrina thanked Martha for her good work at finding Mummy's secret room and gave her a little hug.

"Martha I think we might ask Cook if we can have ice-cream for tea. Come on, we will go back downstairs and let Zach's Daddy come up here with Zach. They are going to read Mummy's books while we make some tea for you and Alex."

"Okay. I hope Mummy won't mind!" Martha said.

"Did Mummy show you in here when you were really little, Martha?" Zach asked.

"Yes, she said it was a secret and I had to tell no one. Not even Daddy!"

"It's all right. Mummy won't be cross with you; she would want you to help us. Because these are all your mother's belongings, so they belong to you."

Katrina and Martha walked back down the stairs and were met by Richard and Miles at the yellow room. They stood back and smiled at Martha and Katrina.

"We are just going to see about some afternoon tea, aren't we, Martha?"

Martha nodded as she and Katrina left them and walked back down to the nursery. From there they picked up Alex, who was now awake and getting a bottle. They took the stairs again and reached the ground floor where they went in search of the cook. Sheila had just finished making some pikelets and was covering them with hot jam.

"Looks like we are just in time for tea, Martha!" Abbey said.

"I have made you some pikelets, scones and chocolate cake. I thought we could have a special tea tonight instead of meat and vegetables for the children," Sheila called out from the pantry.

"What an excellent idea, Sheila. This really looks yummy, doesn't it, Martha?" Kat said.

Katrina and Abbey helped the children with their tea before getting them bathed and ready for bed. Once the two children were fast asleep they came back downstairs to find Aaron, Jared and Craig arriving back from their day away. They had all disappeared early that morning with one of the security guards to pack up Abbeys unit. After all the problems and heartache over Katrina's disappearance they were taking no more chances and the two girls were going nowhere, so the brothers had gone to the unit and sorted through everything up that morning. They had already booked a local removalist and Abbey's belongings were now safely on their way back to Twin Hills.

Abbey's job had also finished abruptly; she had given two weeks' notice and only worked the first week, with everything happening: Katrina's horrible kidnapping and poor Robert's brutal beating. Aaron rang the hospital, complaining she had a high temperature and that he was taking her to the doctor. After that she never returned.

At dinner time that evening there was still no sign of Zach, Richard or Miles. They must have stayed up in Louisa's office trying to sort out the paperwork or maybe trying to read some of the journals. Katrina closed her eyes and contacted Zach. She spoke to him in her mind and he answered "Well, you are never going to believe all the news we have just unearthed," he said.

"Okay. Can you all come down for dinner, poor Sheila is getting worried she is going to burn something."

"We're on our way."

Ten minutes later they were all sitting down for dinner. Miles had found some red and white wine from the cellar and was serving it into the cut crystal, while Sheila was serving the meal out to everyone, which tonight happened to be lasagne and a green side salad. The nine of them sat around the table and made small talk until they finished the meal. Miles and Sheila had trouble sitting down with them, after spending so many years always looking after their guests it was built into them. They would have been happy to eat in the kitchen, however Richard would not hear of it.

"You are part of our team and family, and we work and eat together."

They sat down together and that was it.

"Okay, people, we have a lot to discuss. First of all, we need to arrange a funeral for poor Robert and his mother. We have checked all records and it seems that they were the only family these two beautiful children had. Now before Katrina says anything – and I can feel she is going to, because I know my daughter – we will fight for custody and take them back to Thistle Ridge with us. We need to keep them as safe as possible and knowing what we have found out today, they have to be kept very safe," Richard said.

"Did Robert make a will?" Craig asked.

"If he did it's not here. Miles has gone through his office today and found a lot of bank statements and accounts, but nothing referring to a will. I would say if he made one, which I hope and pray he did, it will be with a solicitor, which is another thing we will check on tomorrow," Richard said.

"What about his mother, did she have anyone?" asked Aaron.

"Mrs Saunders had a boyfriend called Alan, who loved her dearly. She visited here a couple of times last year with him, so we might need to check on him," said Miles.

"I am assuming the police have already been in touch with him. I really hope so! Otherwise it's left to us, and that doesn't seem right," Richard said.

"Okay. Tomorrow we will try and find out all we can from the police, about the boyfriend and see when they will release the bodies for burying. Then we will possibly have to wait until Monday to speak to a solicitor, to see what Robert has instructed in his will.

Robert's funeral will be a huge one as he was in the public eye and had thousands of fans. I can see a cathedral service with thousands of mourners and then maybe a private service for the children at a local crematorium," Richard said.

"Richard, can you tell us what you found out about the children's mother?" Katrina asked.

"Well, it is a long story, which of course I won't go into in depth. But as far as we know without sitting down and reading the journals from cover to cover, we found out that our Louisa was born around 1750 and she received her first journal at the age of fifteen. We found her first journal dated 1765. In that, she says her parents were very excited that at her next birthday in which she would be sixteen years of age, there were two suitors who had spoken to her father and offered to marry her, once she was of age. The first gentleman was charming and very kind, and a lot older than her, maybe ten years. He could give her a lovely house and lots of money. The other gentleman, although very good looking, was from a huge family and around her same age but nowhere near as wealthy. He seemed mean and wanted her as a cook for his large family and a worker."

"Her father decided on her sixteenth birthday that she would go to the first man, the caring older gentleman, who wanted her for companionship and to love and become his wife. They were married and a year later she became pregnant with their first child. They adored each other and spending every moment together could not believe when she suddenly became very sick and was having trouble carrying the baby. She went to full term but with complications and after the baby boy was delivered, she collapsed, dying and we don't know why.

"The husband was immortal and had been living on the earth for over a thousand years. He had never met anyone like Louisa and she was destined to be his mate. He could not let her die, so he transferred some of his blood to her. When she recovered she was told by the doctor, or what they had back then, that she was no longer able to have children and if she did, at any time, she would die. We think that maybe after two hundred and sixty-four years she may have forgotten and was lucky to have Martha but wanted another boy and it was too much for her," Richard said.

Everyone look shocked and speechless, what could anyone say after that?

Sheila asked, "Will they live that long as well or will the blood have diluted down through the mother?"

"Good question, Sheila, but we don't know yet," Zach said.

"That's why you don't want them to leave us, isn't it?" asked Katrina.

"Yes, and no. We can't let these children go to welfare or foster care, they may be walking around with immortal blood inside them. The other reason is they are wealthy in their own right and the government would take all that money if they become wards of the state. There would be nothing left. Their father's money would be in the millions, let alone their mother's, who at more than two hundred years old would have saved a small amount by now. Anyway, if the government know how much these kids are worth they will take it for themselves and the children will be no wiser. We need to look after these children and later, when they are old enough, give them back the money in a trust fund or something," Richard said.

"Do we know what happened to her first husband?" Aaron asked.

"No, we don't know what happened to her first husband. That will probably be in the journals, which we will need to read," Zach said.

There was a slight noise from the front of the house and all the lights went on. The garden lights, the house outside lights, the huge spot lights; it looked like a football stadium. They all left their seats and went out into the hallway.

"Someone is trying to break in," Katrina whispered.

"I see what you mean about the lights now, Kat!" Zach said, hugging her to his side. The security guards were wrestling someone on the grass. Miles and Richard went out to see who it was.

"It's a bloody newspaper reporter trying to get some photos!" the security guard said.

"Okay, call the police and let them take him. We want him charged. How dare he come in here trespassing," Richard called out to them.

"No worries, matie, I will just write the story as I see it," the journalist said, with some of his face still pushed in the grass. Zach went a little closer to read his mind and then came back and said something to his father. Richard asked the guards to bring him into the house but to still call the police. They pushed him down in one of the lounge chairs in the day room.

"Ladies, you don't need to hang around, we can sort this troublemaker out," Richard said.

"We know when we are not needed to do the interrogating!" Abbey said.

"Looks like we get left with the washing up! Again," Katrina said walking out the door and shutting it.

Once they were back in the dining room and Richard could hear the dishes being stacked up, he turned and asked the journalist what he meant.

"Well, it's obvious isn't it? Robert had a run in with his ex-manager over not being paid enough. So he comes round here, with some muscle and beats him up, then to top it off they kill his mother and kidnap the nanny and one of his kids."

"So what are you going to write in your paper? Mr ...?" Zach asked.

"Cannon! The name's Mick Cannon. Well, of course, the truth, mate. That's what the people want to hear!" Cannon said.

"So why do I have a feeling you are thinking of writing a love story, about the rock star and a nanny falling in love and then the rock star dying?" Zach asked.

"How the hell did you do that?"

"It's a gift I have, but there's no way you are going to write that shit. I won't allow it, we won't allow it," Zach said.

"No, that's right. There's no way my daughter is going to be subjected to any more hurt," Richard said.

"That goes for me as well. My sister has been through enough hell. I really don't think you have an option," Jared said.

"You can't stop me!"

Zach turned around to the security guards and asked them to wait outside. Once the door was closed he spoke to Cannon, getting his attention and eye contact. As Zach's eyes started to glow yellow, Cannon's eyes glazed over and he went into a trance. This is what we want to write: 'Robert Saunders, an outstanding rock singer and father of two beautiful children, Martha, three and Alex, 18 months old, has regrettably died in hospital at the age of 29, after receiving a horrific assault from his ex-manager. We gather from the police officers working on the case, that there was a confrontation between the two men. When Evans and his bouncers left the Saunders home that afternoon, there was one family member dead at the scene, with Saunders himself fighting for his life.

"The children are now in care of relatives who have travelled far to be with them and ask for some privacy while they help the children with their devastating loss." Zach said.

"I think that should be enough, don't you, Cannon?" Richard asked.

"Very good, sir, I will get right on to it," Cannon said, grabbing his note pad off Richard.

"Hopefully you can read my writing?" Richard said.

The journalist was escorted outside for the security guards to dispose of.

Zach found Katrina in the kitchen talking to the ladies. He went over and whispered in her ear and then took her by the hand. "Good night ladies." Abbey and Sheila laughed and said goodnight.

Once he had Kat back securely in her little home he pulled her to him and kissed her passionately. When they broke apart, breathing heavily, Katrina looked up and asked him. "What's wrong, did something go wrong in there?"

"No, it's been taken care of. He should be safely on his way back to work to write his article, with the aid of a lift from the police officers."

"So what's wrong, I can feel it?"

"I have something for you and I wanted to give it you in private."

"Didn't you give me that this morning?"

"No, not that!" he said laughing. "This is what I wanted to give you. I am sorry it's taken so long but they had to track down the right colour stones." He pulled out of his pocket a small square box. Katrina's heart started to beat fast, she was suddenly very nervous. He knelt down on the carpet and asked, "I know we have already become true mates but I wanted to ask you to be my wife. I love you so much, with all my heart and I never want to be apart from you, it hurts too much. You are part of my soul now and forever."

Katrina held back the tears, she couldn't have been happier.

"I love you so much, in this form and the other. I would love to be your wife."

He opened the box and handed it to her. She looked down and found inside the most beautiful ring she had ever seen. The ring had a large freeform parti-colour sapphire in a step cut which seemed to be very natural and in yellow and green. On either side were two emerald cut diamonds glistening on a yellow gold band. Beside it was a narrower gold band, encrusted with diamonds and yellow and green sapphires. She looked up at him and the tears started to roll down her face. He stepped forward and wiped the tears away from her cheeks and said, "It was supposed to make you happy, not sad."

"It's the most beautiful thing I have ever received and I will cherish it all my life."

"The ring was designed with you and me in mind. The yellow sapphires are my eyes and the green ones are yours, together they will always be together on your wedding ring. The engagement ring is a green and yellow parti sapphire, very hard to find, from Rubyvale. It combines our eye colours as well. So together on your finger there will always be a reminder of you and me, together."

"Will you put the engagement ring on for me?" asked Kat.

"I would like nothing better. I want the world to know you belong to me and no one else." He slid the ring on to her finger and kissed her.

"I love them both, when did you have time to pick them up?"

"I didn't have time Jared did it. He was happy to go into the city for me. The jewellers rang the other day and said they had finished putting the last of the sapphires into the wedding ring."

"Wow, that was nice of him."

"He would do anything for you!"

"Yes, it's good having a brother. I love that family so much. They were always there for me. I really hope he will be able to find someone special like I have, who will truly love him too."

Zach led Katrina upstairs and into the bedroom, where he slowly undressed her, dumping clothes in a pile by the bed. Zach then walked her into the bathroom and ran a hot shower which he knew she would love after the exhausting day they had both had. After washing each other all over, they moved back to the bedroom and made love. There was nothing to interrupt them tonight and they could forget about the last few days. They were both together, bonded with their bodies and souls.

Chapter 12

By Wednesday of the following week Richard had spoken to the police and found out that they would release the bodies by the end of the week. The police had informed them that they had been in touch with Mrs Saunders's boyfriend, Alan. He would be flying over to pick up her body and take her back to Perth.

Mrs Saunders had always told him that she never wanted to leave the coastal city and so he was arranging a quiet funeral for close friends and some of his family.

Robert's funeral was going to be a different matter; the local government in Brisbane had decided they would take over the arrangements as he was a local icon. So all Zach and his family had to do was show up with the children on the right day, at the right time.

Cannon had not disappointed anyone and had written a lovely piece about Robert, his career, and young family in the Sunday Mail that night; it was breaking hearts all over the state.

The funeral had been set for the following Monday morning, at 10.30am. They were expecting fans to come from all over the country to pay their respects. It seemed like it was turning into a state funeral instead of a humble passing.

Martha had been told by Zach and Katrina that Daddy had been very sick and was now in heaven with Mummy and that they watching over her and Alex. She seemed to understand but the poor child was only three, after all.

When Miles had gone upstairs into Robert's bedroom with the cleaner, he'd found an address book by his bedside cabinet. It revealed the contacts that they were looking for; the solicitor, his new manager, his accountant and bank manager.

When Richard called the solicitor they had already heard the news, they asked that Katrina Cross and Miles Stewart come to their office on Friday at 2pm.

On Friday morning Katrina was a bag of nerves; she had never been into a solicitor's office before. It had something to do with Robert's will, but she was really at an end, not knowing. She thought because Miles was going that maybe they had been left some jobs, like selling the house or something.

Katrina thought that if he had made the will before his mother's death, maybe they were supposed to go and live with Mrs Saunders.

Or maybe his mother was going to be asked to come here, with the children. They only had to wait around for another three hours and then they would know.

When two o'clock arrived Katrina and Miles stood outside the entrance of Bookman and Sultana Solicitors. They both took deep breaths and walked into the offices. They were greeted by a well-groomed lady in a black suit who showed them into the nearby office. They were met by Mr Sultana, who was in his late fifties and smartly dressed in what looked like an Armani suit. He was obliviously loaded and with the clientèle, who could blame him? He walked over and shook their hands and asked them to have a seat. Katrina took another deep breath and sat down next to Miles.

"Thank you both for coming. We are truly shocked and mourning the loss of Mr Saunders here in this office and our deepest sympathy goes to you both. He was the kindest man I know and being a huge celebrity star didn't change him at all. He was a very clever and talented man, when it came to writing lyrics for the band. Robert will be dearly missed and there are thousands of fans probably feeling the same way and mourning him as we speak.

"Again, I am sorry for your loss and will try not to keep you too long and will let you know what he has instructed."

"Thank you, Mr Sultana, it has been devastating for the whole family and the poor children are really too young to know that they have lost both their parents," Miles said.

"I want you to know that if there is anything, I can do for you, you must let us know. We are here to help you with any problems. We have also been instructed to help you further and look after the children's inheritance, which we can go over at another time.

"Robert had instructed us to ask you, Miles Stewart, to be the executor of the will. He has asked that if anything happened to him, you would look after the money side of things. He says that because he has known you for over fifteen years, he could think of no one better to do the job. He has asked that the children be educated in the best schools growing up and then if required, they both go on to university.

"He has requested that you be paid an excellent wage to cover yourself and for overseeing the children.

"However, Robert has said if you do not wish to stay with the children, we are to cover all your expenses and requests that you be paid a lump sum for all your trouble. We will need to get signatures from both of you for opening bank accounts, etc. There is also a small envelope for Sheila Bevans, that we have been asked to give to you."

"Thank you, I will pass it on to her," Miles said.

"To Katrina Cross, whom I hold very dear in my heart, I have left my children, Alex Marc Saunders and Martha Louisa Saunders. She is the only one I care enough about, who would love them like I do and look after them. If my mother is still alive, I know she's going to be upset and angry but Katrina is the only one who I trust with their safety and who will teach them well, with the guidance of Miles overseeing them.

"Katrina Cross is also to be paid a large salary which is written down, so that she will never be in need of anything for herself or the children. I understand that she is still young and I hope that the children will not be too much of a burden on her."

By the time the solicitor had finished reading out the will, Katrina was a mess. The tears were running down her face and she could not believe this was actually happening. Miles sat close squeezing her hand, trying to comfort her.

Katrina was so happy that the children would be safe with them, but also very sad that poor Robert had been taken so young. He had been a good man, looking after all his staff and caring for them both and his children.

As well, he had wanted to share his life with the children, taking them and her on organised rock concert tours. Really, no one deserved to die that way.

Miles and Katrina walked out of the office an hour later in tears and shaken by the news. They were met outside by Richard and Zach, who immediately took Katrina into his arms. She was still shaking and his strong embrace helped her to calm down.

"Well, how did you go?" Richard asked.

"I can't believe it, but I have been left the children with a salary that is truly mental. It is supposed to help me with anything I would need for myself or the children. The children also have their own allowance," Katrina said, sobbing into poor Zach's shirt.

"Well that's good, isn't it? That's what we all wanted!" Zach said.

"Yes but Miles didn't really get to say whether he wanted to stay or go."

"Katrina, it's all right," Miles said.

"Miles has been requested to be the executor of all finances to oversee the funeral and the will. He has been instructed to oversee the care of the children, through schooling and college or university" Kat said.

"Katrina, it's not as bad as you think. We would have come with you. Sheila and I. We decided that a few days ago, there's nothing here if the children are gone and starting off with another family would be too much hassle now, as we are both getting older. I know your family have special gifts and there's different things happening around us that we don't understand, but we really want to be a part of it. Wherever you go, we want to be near," Miles said.

"We were hoping you would stay with us, Miles. We will explain everything later when we get home. Away from the public eye, there are too many ears and eyes in this town," said Zach.

"As I said the other night, you are part of the family, we need you. You are just going to have to get used to being part of a different family, that's all," Richard said.

"Sheila and I are both open minded. Will you have enough accommodation for all of us? Your family has just increased by four."

"Good job for the cabins," Kat said.

"Yes, we might have to get some more ordered. Or maybe extend the house again, but there's no problem. We all go together," Richard said.

"Okay, Richard. I would like to suggest that we hire a storage container and clear the house of all the children's belongings and any family heirlooms and let out the house. In that way, we can keep it if the children ever want to come back to it later," Miles said.

"That sounds like a good plan. Let's get out of here and see what we can organise. We can check on what's happening with Robert's funeral at the same time," Richard said.

They left the solicitor's office and made their way back to the children's home.

When they arrived at the main entrance, they were met by several television crews and mourners putting flowers, cards and posters for Robert along the wall by the large gates at the entrance. The camera crews all changed their directions, trying to film them in the car, instead of the mourners. Even the mourners stopped to look at them, watching them drive through the gates into the property. Katrina suddenly felt sickened, she had never been one for the spotlight. Remembering how very hard it was going to be on Monday at the funeral.

Through dinner that evening they discussed in detail the solicitor's meeting. What ideas they all had and which ones they needed to work on. They discussed how they should go through the funeral arrangements, until everyone knew what their jobs would entail.

Alan had called in on the Saturday morning to pay his respects and to see them all before returning to Perth with Mrs Saunders's body. The meeting was so very sad but he seemed a little happier after meeting them all and had promised to keep in contact with them.

Over the weekend Miles and Richard worked together to organise several real estate agents to come and view the property. They arrived throughout the weekend at scheduled times, and all of them with high interest in either selling the property for them or leasing it out. Miles had asked for it to be leased at the moment, as there was rush to do anything; it was the children's home and they might want to return to it.

There were several real estate agents that were helpful, but one in particular, a Mr Jenkins, had suggested that they leased the home semi-furnished. By leaving some of the main rooms with the basic furniture in, it made it more appealing to the tenant. He walked around with Miles and pointed out ideas. He suggested leaving the dining room with its twelve-seated heavy oak dining table and chairs and its matching huge wooden dresser. He also suggested the lounge furniture in the both the day rooms. It had been tastefully picked with the house in mind. The theatre room with all the high-tech surround sound and movie watching equipment and maybe leave a couple of bedrooms furnished, from which there were ample to choose.

It was left to Mr Jenkins to follow through with all the paperwork and find the right tenant.

All the personal items, like Robert's musical instruments, his writing desk and bedroom furniture, all his books and photographs would be packed away in a furniture storage container for later when the children were older. Katrina had asked that all the furniture from Louisa's hidden room be all stored away as well, with Robert's. She had also asked that Martha had the furniture from the yellow bedroom as she thought Louisa might have picked it with her daughter in mind, for when she grew up later. It, too, would be stored away for later. That left the three apartments of the staff to be packed up, of all of the furnishings. It would come in handy for the move to Thistle Ridge. The cellar needed to be emptied of wine and packed to take with them, and the kitchen of all Sheila's belongings and the equipment that had been bought for her by Robert.

Through the weekend Katrina had picked up a few things that she wanted to take back for the children now, which included some photos of the children's parents and some of Robert with his band and others of just Robert and the children. She thought they would be able to go onto the walls in the children's bedroom when they worked out where everyone was going to live.

On Monday morning Katrina woke early after a night with very little sleep. She had been rest less and on edge since the visit to the solicitors on the Friday. She had been dreading the funeral and didn't like the idea of exposing the children to public view. She had also seen some of the news reports suggesting than there must have been something going on with Robert and the nanny for Robert to leave the children in her care.

Carl, the head man and leader of the crows' shifter flock, had come up with a beautiful plan to put the reporters on to something else and keep them away from Katrina and the rest of the royal family. He had introduced one of his shifters, who happened to be a crow and a very stunning looking female. She was called Annette and was the sort of girl Robert would be seen with in a restaurant or nightclub. Attracting looks where ever she went, she was gorgeous with very long legs, wavy blonde hair and sparkling blue eyes. She had visited the home with Carl and it was arranged between

Carl and Richard that she would be seen at the funeral, making a fuss of Katrina and the children. They needed to squash any speculation, for the newspapers and TV reporters.

At 10 am three black limousines came and picked them up. Katrina had made sure that there were child seats aboard. The children were dressed in dark clothes and sat in the front car with Katrina, Zach and Richard. They were followed by Craig, Jared, Miles and Sheila in the next car and then Abbey, Aaron and the two security guards in the last one.

The drivers took them to the side entrance of St. Joseph's Cathedral. They all climbed out and Kat gave Zach little Martha to hold on to while she grabbed the baby. The driver brought around the pram and held on to it while she strapped in the baby. Alex could still look around or go to sleep if he wished. Sheila arrived with the baby's bag full of soft toys and a few snacks, to keep him quiet through the service.

They were escorted inside and given seats at the front of the church, before the pulpit. Jared, Craig and the two security guards stood nearby, keeping watch and making sure no one attempted to get within a metre of any of them. Martha had been given Katrina's iPad and she was happy watching *Toy Story 2* again. The congregation were already piling in with stewards showing them where to find their seats. It looked like it had been well organised. The coffin was brought in and the whole place went quiet, except little Martha who looked up at Katrina and said very quietly, "Is that where Daddy is?" Katrina, Sheila and half the congregation were sobbing. Katrina tried to smile at her and was so relieved when Richard stood up and picked Martha up, taking her back to his seat.

Annette was one of the last to walk in with Carl and some of the shifters. She walked over to Katrina and hugged her. There was a slight shushing in the cathedral from the congregation and a few camera shots been taken, and then it went quiet as the bishop came out.

The rest of the service went past in a daze to Katrina and she was happy when Zach touched her on the cheek, bringing her back to the present and telling her it all over.

Zach squeezed her hand as they stood up to meet the bishop, with the rest of the family. Richard carried Martha outside to the waiting limousine and strapped her in. As Katrina pushed a chattering Alex out of the cathedral. She smiled, chattering back at him, he had been so good all the way through the service. She had been amazed and was so grateful.

As she too climbed into the car she noticed for the first time, all the activity around her. There were camera crews everywhere with the journalists talking into microphones. One crew belonging to Channel 7 had Robert's band members and were asking them questions. Another crew were chasing Annette and Carl down the street, as they walked away.

Katrina sat back, relaxing a little with Zach as the car started to move away. She noticed it was only her and Zach.

"Where's Richard?"

"He's going on to the crematorium with Miles and Sheila. He had arranged this so we could go back to the house with the children and the security guards. He didn't seem to think they needed to see any more."

"Oh, that is wonderful news; I really didn't know how I was going to get through that. I don't think the crematorium is a place for children and I am sure Robert wouldn't want his children there," Kat said.

When they arrived back at the main gates, Katrina spotted trucks parked at the back of the property with 'Bite Me' Catering written on them. She looked over at Zach and asked him through her mind, "What's all this for?"

"Well, we have to give a small wake to the members of the band, some of the other celebrities that knew him well, the mayor and some of the council officials. Some other bigwigs from God knows where. Blah! Blah! I think there's about eighty booked for lunch, but we are not having it inside, it will be in the marquee at the back."

"Well at least poor Sheila does not have to cook, that would be a nightmare after today."

"No way! Dad said we would get the outside caterers in to start with. It cannot be easy on those guys either, they have just lost their boss. Poor Miles has been with Robert for fifteen years and Sheila at least five. Robert's mother employed him to look after Robert at the age of 12 and it would have really hit him hard to lose both of them. Especially in that way."

"Oh! Poor Miles, he must be truly cracking up, underneath his controlled appearance!" Kat said.

"He is trained from an early age, to be a butler. His job is to serve and to do what is requested but never to question. His job is to serve everyone before he serves himself. He will never let emotion get in the way of his duty," Zach said.

"Wow! I had no idea, I was just moping around, feeling sorry for myself and the children," Kat said.

"It's your way of coping with the grief. His will be totally different. You may never see his other side but I am hoping we can pull it out of him."

"Okay, so what is required of us at this luncheon?"

"We are to mingle and talk to people I will be beside you at all times. There will be no journalists or camera crews getting in and we have extra security guards on the gates and around the house and gardens. Abbey, Jared and Aaron will be keeping watch on the children so you can relax a little, so there will be no worries of children saying anything awkward, not that that was bad in the church."

"She just said what anyone would ask if they didn't know," Katrina said.

"I know, sweetheart, it's okay! Another few hours and we should be packing up to go home."

"I haven't seen my parents since I was kidnapped and they are really anxious to see me. They are going to be surprised that we have collected a ready-made family. Lucky you proposed, ah!"

"Yes, I think I scored well!"

"I am still amazed that I even got your attention, being such a hot sexy guy that you are."

"I really love the way that you think you don't look hot. You should have heard what my brothers said the night you walked into the pub. They both thought you were something special, it was only when I started to growl at them both, that they pulled their heads in and apologised."

"I thought I heard someone growl, but no one else in the bar seemed to hear it and I thought maybe I had been hearing things."

"No, that was me and you only heard because you were destined to be my mate. From that moment on,

215

whether you wanted it or not you were able to tune into me. When I used to visit you at night once you had gone to bed at the hotel, you always seemed to know when I was coming. You would always have the curtains drawn back and would be sitting on the window sill waiting for me."

"Well I wished I had remembered by the morning, because I was really starting to think I was going loopy. The first two nights at the hotel I would draw the curtains at night to find them wide opened when I woke up in the morning. I could not for the life of me remember what happened the night before."

"That was probably me helping with that. I really needed you to know me first, before I showed you the griffin but the griffin would not relax until he had seen you for himself, so we waited until everyone had gone to bed before flying up to your room and visiting you," Zach said.

"I can see why Jared went off at you when he first met you. Because you could have done anything you wanted to me and I would not have known anything about it," she said.

"Yes, he really is too smart that guy for his own good."

"Not so! I think he was protecting my dignity and other bits and pieces," she said laughing.

"Well, I want to see those other bits and pieces but I am afraid they will have to wait until after this luncheon party that we are giving in memory of Robert. But I won't forget and my griffin won't forget either," he said laughing.

The luncheon started about 1.30pm when everyone had arrived back from the crematorium. It went for a few hours and then they were able to return inside. Katrina went to check on the children before starting some more packing. Abbey and Aaron had everything under control and were all sat down, relaxing and watching a *Postman Pat* video.

Miles had the removalists arriving at seven thirty in the morning to empty the three apartments, of all furniture and knick-knacks. Most of the small things had already been boxed up and it was just the heavy things left.

Between Katrina and Miles, they had decided they would be taking everything that belonged to the children, back to Thistle Ridge. Which meant all the nursery equipment, book cases, high chairs, a couple of portable cots, games, toys and other essentials like change tables and baby gates. They were taking all the furniture from both of the children's bedrooms, as they had nothing where they were heading. Katrina had decided to decorate the children's rooms the same as they were at their home, hoping it would help the children settle in quicker.

Sheila had been packing her kitchen up and was leaving the bare essentials for the tenants. She was hoping that she would be able to carry on catering for everyone when she and Miles arrived at Thistle Ridge.

Katrina had mentioned to Sheila that her parents ran a hotel and it was the only place to eat in town. So there was always cooking that needed doing there and then maybe her mother could take it a little easier. She could not remember the last time her parents had taken a holiday. She would definitely suggest that they both took a holiday, once she had the children settled back there.

Robert's personal belongings, his office furniture, bedroom furniture, instruments, books and mementos would be professional packed up to go into storage. The removalists had a large shed complex where the containers were stored in a dry environment once everything had been packed away and the container locked. It would then stay there until it was needed later.

Jared and Craig had taken Katrina's little Pulsar into the city and exchanged it for a brand new four-wheel drive. (A deep blue, Toyota Hi-lux dual cab.)

Although she would not be driving home, one of the brothers would be taking it back for her. She would be taking the direct route and flying straight home with the children in the helicopter, with Zach and Richard.

Katrina would now have transport when she arrived back in her home town, to be independent and not worry about grabbing lifts.

By Tuesday lunch time the removalists were in full swing. They had completely emptied the staff apartments, the nursery and were loading up the children's bedrooms onto the truck. Another group of men had carefully wrapped up all Robert's belongings and were packing them into a storage container.

Miles and Sheila were going to stay until everything was all done, and they were both happy to leave their old home in the hands of the real estate. As their own furniture had been packed onto the truck they decided to move into one of the four guest bedrooms, which had been left fully furnished in the main house. Together they would oversee the rest of the packing and the cleaning of all the rooms and staff quarters before they left to head out to their new home.

The rest of them would be leaving in a convoy of cars today. Jared and Craig had been asked to take Katrina's new car back and Aaron and Abbey were driving Robert's BMW, which had been left to Miles. They were arranging between themselves where they were going to meet up for the night. Craig had told Zach they would head in land from Brisbane and stop at Roma for the night and then continue through to Emerald and then on to Twin Hills the next day. As there were two drivers in each car they could share the driving.

Zach was driving the hire car back to the airport to drop it off and then leaving in the helicopter, with the children, Richard and Katrina. He was hoping to get them all home before nightfall, he could fly in the dark but it would be easier for the children if it was still daylight when they arrived home.

After everyone said their goodbyes they all parted company and headed for their destinations.

Zach dropped Richard and Katrina with the children, bags and car seats at the departure lounge and went and parked the hire car. After standing in the queue for ten minutes and then getting severely questioned by the receptionist, as to why a different driver happened to be bringing back the car and not one of the drivers that had taken the vehicle, the paperwork was somehow finalised and they were able to leave.

By late afternoon they were landing on the helicopter pad behind the house, to a waiting, cheering crowd of flock and pack members, surrounding Zach's mum. It was so good to see their home again and Katrina thought after all the trouble she had been through the last few weeks. She decided at that moment she never wanted to leave again. Once the helicopter blades stopped and they all climbed out, they were truly welcomed back, receiving hugs and kisses, even the children who hadn't met any of them before were suddenly passed around and hugged as well. They were later carried inside and settled in another room with two or three pack members fussing over them. It was the first time they were able to relax and unwind from the last few days. Katrina loved the way Richard kept hugging and kissing his wife, he too showed a lot of emotion and love for his beautiful wife.

A large barbeque was organised for the evening and they were going to do the same tomorrow night, when the rest of the family arrived. Amy had brought some wine over and sat down next to Katrina. She squeezed her hand and said, "It's so good to see you back home here, safe and sound. We were really panicking here when we heard you and little Alex had been kidnapped. I kept thinking I should never have let you go after the night you got the shits with Zach and Richard and left so abruptly."

"I am sorry about that! I really am, I just have always been so headstrong and independent. I get it from my father and being a redhead I suppose doesn't help. It's just that I had a plan, growing up, for a great career and to see the world, to leave here and go to the big city. I had no need to worry about anyone else, just myself. But over the last few months my life has so dramatically changed. I now have a wonderful partner who I love with all my heart. I have inherited two beautiful children at the age of nearly twenty-three, and I am back where I started. So in fact I have completed a full circle," Kat said.

"Well, I am so glad that we will be here to share it with you. You have given my son so much, it's just wonderful to see him so very happy. I was so worried for him. More for him than the other two boys, because he will need to be strong later when Richard retires. It will be Zach who will need to lead the flock and pack and the way our numbers are increasing I don't know how many that will be. It's good he has you, to stand by him and give him the strength and support he needs," Amy said.

"Did they tell you about the children and how we think they have special gifts?" Katrina asked.

"Yes, I think it's amazing! And I can't wait to spend some time with them."

"Have my parents rung you at all?"

"Yes, they have and I let them know that you were hoping to fly back this afternoon," Amy said.

"Oh, good. I'll try and get over there tomorrow and see them. I know they have been a little out of touch with what's been happening as I can only tell them so much!"

"Well, I think that might change, Richard asked Miles and Sheila to come back with you. Once they know, I don't see why your parents cannot know, they will be family after all. Also they are going to be around a lot of shifters from now on so I think it only makes sense."

The men came walking into the lounge, Zach holding Martha upside down and Richard carrying the baby.

"The children will be sleeping in the office in our suite, Kat, until we can prepare something a little more substantial. Martha has a mattress on the floor and Alex is in the portable cot until the furniture arrives tomorrow. Suzie has volunteered to read them a story after their tea and bath time. They have just come in to say goodnight and we are going to take them back to our rooms and then we can relax with you guys," Zach said.

"I can come and help you do that," Katrina said.

"Yes, we know, but we're going to do it tonight, you sit down and relax with Mum," Zach said as he put a wriggling Martha on Katrina's lap.

"I will be in later, sweetie, to kiss you good night."

"Good night, Trina," Martha said as she gave her one last kiss before Zach picked her up and threw her over his shoulder.

"God! Please tell me she hasn't had tea yet, she will throw up all down your back, Zach!" Katrina said.

"Listen to our new mother! Ah! Dad!" The men walked away, laughing between themselves.

Chapter 13

Over the next month two large two-bedroom log cabins had been erected in between the tree lines behind the main homestead. Sheila and Miles were moving into one permanently with their own furniture from their apartments in Brisbane. The other one was being left for visiting guests like her parents and housed most of Katrina's furniture from her apartment. Miles and Sheila no longer had to hide their relationship as they did under Robert's employment and were happy to live together. Robert had insisted with his children around, that everything was done properly. He was very old fashioned and didn't even bring females home to sleep with, he would take them to a hotel or somewhere else.

Miles had relaxed a lot since arriving and seemed to have dropped a lot of the high-class formalities, but he was still a butler no one could ever change that. They had both been welcomed by the rest of the flock and after a few days it was like they had always been there.

When Miles and Sheila first decided all those weeks ago, after Robert's death, to stay with Katrina and the children Richard had asked them to come out and relax and be there for the children. But slowly they had wormed their way into the royal household, with Sheila taking over a lot of the cooking for Amy and all the other residents. She had also gone in a few times to the hotel with Katrina to help Mary cook for large functions.

Katrina's parents were very happy to see their daughter return to Twin Hills and were so excited to meet their new grandchildren. Katrina had rung them when she returned after the kidnapping to let them know all the news. She had also rung them again and cried down the phone when she broke the news of Robert's death.

Charlie and Mary had both wanted to fly down to her aid but she had insisted that there was nothing they could do. Zach was taking good care of her and not letting her out of his sight. She told them that they would be home as soon as they could and once there, she and Zach would not be travelling out of the area in a hurry.

She had told them that her main priority was to help organise the funeral and then go with Miles to fight the solicitors to keep the children together and bring them back to Thistle Ridge with them. Only when she when she rang them the next time it was to tell them what had happened to her and Miles at the solicitors. They could not believe that their daughter had, at twenty-two suddenly become a mother of two orphaned children. Charlie and Mary had been told a little about the Williams curse or gift, depending how you perceived it, after the family had arrived back to Twin Hills. Richard and Amy had gone over to the hotel one night for dinner with Katrina and Zach. Zach had been there to help them forget if it went bad and they screamed and shouted in hysteria. Only when they were told, they both had gone very quiet, each one absorbing the information. Zach could sense there was something that Charlie and Mary weren't telling them. They didn't seem to be freaked out or disappointed that their only daughter was marrying a shifter. It was something else entirely.

There was plenty to do around the place. Miles was kept busy organising his designs for more extensions on the house. The builders were due in after the wedding, to start knocking down walls again. They had decided that Zach and Katrina's suite needed to be extended, with at least another two bedrooms added and a nursery. Katrina had said that she would have been happy living in a log cabin, but Richard wouldn't hear of it, he'd said.

"They're all right for a night or two, but you need space, not a box, to live in with those children. It will drive you nuts."

So Miles had designed it so that when the builders came they would mirror the effect onto Aaron's rooms, as he and Abbey would be moving in together and later on maybe having children of their own.

Aaron had moved out temporarily and given his rooms to Miles and Sheila. He and Abbey had decided they needed some privacy to start their relationship and had moved in to the log cabin next to the wishing well. They had decided that they would take over from Zach and Katrina and continue working down at Black Boulders. They were adding to the gardens and making room for six stables, which they were going to build, and a round yard.

Abbey was travelling backwards and forwards to her parents' station, where Jared and Andy had managed to get hold of some wild brumbies. They made good rides once they were broken in, and there was a wide range of ages in the group of twelve horses they had captured. The brothers never disclosed where they found the pack of horses but Abbey had some idea, and it wasn't near their land. She knew her brothers went far and wide in flight sometimes, although they weren't supposed to. They knew to stay on their own land in case humans spotted them and freaked out, but her brothers did like to break the rules sometimes.

Abbey had picked three mares and a quiet looking mare with a foal on the ground, which she thought would be good for a beginner. Several older looking colts would need to be gelded and the rest they could play with later.

Zach and Richard had both been shocked to see that there were more shifters living in Australia, than they knew about. Some breeds, like the werewolves, they had no idea even lived here and Mr and Mrs. Donohue had immigrated years ago. So they were redoing the database for all shifters living in Australia, it was going to take months but at least they had help, with Carl in Brisbane and the Donohues in Melbourne and their daughter living up in Cairns.

Katrina was as busy as ever with Alex and Martha. Amy had helped her turn one of the original bedrooms Mr Harris had into a nursery. They had set up one of the small TVs that they had brought from Brisbane and a DVD player. Once Martha's favourite video was on, Katrina had time to paint the walls pastel colours and stencilled some pictures, on top of them making it more like a nursery.

When she wasn't looking after the children she had been organising her wedding, which was coming up quicker than she thought it would. Her wedding was next month (November) and she had less than four weeks before she said, 'I do' on November 20th at 3pm.

The mums, Amy and Mary, had been working together since she gave them the date. The wedding invitations had been emailed and mailed out, to both sides of the family. They had sent out over one hundred and fifty invitations. That did not include the flock of around fifty who lived on the property and in town. They had decided to add onto the invitation that if guests wanted to stay they would need to bring their own tents, camping trailers or swags, as the accommodation would be limited, but there would be plenty of portable toilets and showers, and no worries about food.

Katrina had said she would have preferred to get married with just a handful of people. But when she counted her parents, Abbey's family, Zach's family and the children, Miles and Sheila there were seventeen, without the rest of residents living at Thistle Ridge.

But as everyone knows, you always have to invite a long list of people that you don't see from one year to the next to keep the peace, so that's what their mothers were doing. The marquees and portable cold rooms had been booked in for the week of the wedding from Charters Towers. The council were bringing the portable toilets and the shower blocks out from Clermont. The outside catering they were going to do between themselves, with the help of Sheila and Hailey from the hotel.

Katrina had booked the celebrant; it was an old school friend of hers and Abbey's who now lived in Clermont. She had been so excited to hear from Katrina that she wasn't going to charge her. But Katrina talked her out of it, as it was her business and money didn't seem to be a problem with them at the moment.

Her gown was being hand made by one of the ladies in the town. She had been a seamstress all her life and was so excited to be making Katrina's gown. It had been a very hard secret to keep and no one was allowed to know about the dress, even her mother.

Zach could read her mind and anyone else's for that matter, and she did not want him seeing what she was wearing before the day. Every time he had asked her what she had been up to she was giving him a picture in her mind of hanging out washing or vacuuming. Or she pictured herself in a big white fluffy wedding dress. It seemed to be working, because he kept shaking his head at her and laughing.

She had managed to find a lot of the things she needed online, as there were no material shops, clothes or shoe shops close by. She had been lucky with the dressmaker, who had a large selection of pearls and satin beads that she needed for the bodice on her dress.

Her flowers had taken a while to sort out, but the florist had assured her there would be no problems and that she would personally deliver them all, the morning of the wedding, from Charters Towers. Katrina had ordered three bouquets, three simple headdresses, and four wrist posies for Amy, Mary, Sheila and Eileen. Ten large floral decorations, for the reception, and about fifteen rose buttonholes for the men. The florist had also told her that she would bring some extra flowers to make up any buttonholes or table decorations that they had forgotten about. The ring bearer, little Alex, would be wearing black pants and a white winged collared shirt with a matching coloured waistcoat in the same material as the bridesmaids, who would be Martha and Abbey. Abbey had decided on a Christmas wedding. She would have been happy to have a double wedding but after all the nightmare Katrina and the children had been through, it was going to be Katrina's special day and she decided they didn't want to spoil it.

Abbey had also decided that she and Aaron needed a little more time before they made that major step.

Katrina had kept the colour of the bridesmaids' dresses between Abbey, Martha and her mother who had travelled to the dressmaker's with them.

Katrina had picked one of Zach's favourite colours, a pale emerald green, very close to the natural stone in colour. The material was watered taffeta and they had picked a design that could be worn by both Abbey and Martha. As the weather happened to be warming up they decided on a square neckline, no sleeves and a full skirt down to their calves. The girls were indeed going to look lovely.

Katrina's mother had been quiet all the time at the dressmaker's and Katrina was starting to get a little worried.

"Mum, is everything alright? Is there something you don't like about the dresses?"

"Oh, no. Katrina, they are lovely. Sorry, my mind was elsewhere."

"You are going to have to share with me what's wrong!" Kat said.

"I can't, honey, I feel too ashamed. Besides it was years ago and what's done is done!"

"Mum! You are making no sense to me at all!"

The sun was starting to go down as they all left the dressmaker's and as Katrina took her mother back to the hotel Mary said, "Do you want to come in or keep going home?"

"No, Mum, we will keep going. I need to get Martha back for some tea. Thanks anyway, say hi to Dad for me!" She waved to them as they drove off down the road. On the way back to Thistle Ridge she heard Zach calling her.

"Are you all right?" he said inside her head.

"Yes, I am fine, but my mother is still freaking out about something! Do you think Richard might be able to have a talk to her, privately?"

"Yes, I will talk to him; it's obviously something has been stirred up, some old memories maybe, since we told them we were shifters. Maybe Dad, can talk to her, or your dad," Zach said.

"Yes, that must be it! I can remember Mum saying that she had recognised your father on the day of the council's luncheon at the hotel. I can't remember whether she was at school or college with him? She seemed a little disappointed that he had not recognised her."

"Holy Shit! Look out, Kat! What the f... is that?" Abbey screamed.

"What the shit! Zach, are you seeing this?" called Kat.

Katrina pushed the brake pedal right to the floor and the car did an emergency stop. Kangaroos flew past them.

"Martha! Are you all right, honey?"

"What's that?"

"I don't know, honey."

"I will get out and have a look," Abbey said.

"No, you freaking won't. I am not losing you to whatever the hell that is!" Kat shouted.

A bunch of grey and red kangaroos were bouncing and hopping madly in all directions, trying to get the hell away from what was suddenly chasing them. They were not watching the road, all too intent on moving fast. It was getting dark but from what they could see with the lights of the car on, it was huge. It looked to be the size of a horse, only twice as long in the body and standing about three metres high. It had huge feet as it walked across the road and its skin seemed to be scaled and shiny. As it saw the car it stared right at them, flapped its huge black wings and took off after the kangaroos, dragging a large, long tail covered in scales with it.

"No way! It's a fucking dragon!" Katrina shouted.

"Mum said naughty word," Martha squeaked. Katrina and Abbey suddenly looked at each other and laughed hysterically.

"Oh! My goodness, Martha, you called me mum that should be the best moment I could wish for, darling, but I think we need to get the hell out of here," she shouted and took off down the road.

"I second that, where did he suddenly come from? I didn't know they even existed, let alone lived around here!"

"Holy crap! Abbey, how the hell did you make out that was a guy?"

"Well, I didn't. I just thought he looked male."

"Okay! Well I hope I never see him again," Katrina said.

They arrived at the boundary of Thistle Ridge, to be met by oncoming cars. They stopped and climbed out to wait for the oncoming traffic. The stars were out and it was a beautiful night, with just a little chill in the air. Zach rushed over to Katrina and picked her up in a strong embrace, kissing her hard on the mouth. Katrina's arms encircled his neck, loving him back. When they broke apart for a breath Katrina said, "Zach I have only been gone two and a half hours. I should go away more often if I get this attention."

"Kat, you will always get this attention. Now what did you guys see?"

Martha, holding onto Abbey, said, "Mum said rude word!"

231

The whole crowd went quiet.

"What did Mummy say? Martha?"

"She said ucking dragon!" Martha said.

"Did she now? Well Mummy is going to get spanked later, that is very naughty," Zach said, trying to keep a straight face.

"Honey, if you saw a bloody dragon in the middle of nowhere I think you would say the same thing. How long has it been here and how the hell have we never seen it before?" Kat said.

"It was chasing a herd of kangaroos," Abbey said.

"Well, we are just going to have a fly around and see if we pick up any scents."

"I'll come, I haven't been out for a while," Abbey said.

"Okay, all of you stay together. We don't know if this dragon is hostile or not! Please watch each other's backs," Richard called out.

"I will see you in a while, Kat, and don't forget that spanking you will be getting," Zach said, laughing.

"I'll take your clothes with me, and then you will have to come looking for me to get them back," Katrina said in his head.

The shifters all stripped off down to their underwear and shifted into birds of prey and a griffin and took off into the evening skies, leaving Richard, herself and little Martha on the ground watching it all. As Richard was busy sending his sensors out to see if he could pick up anything, Kat decided to load Martha back into the car and to drive up to the homestead.

She was met by Miles, Sheila and Amy, who were watching out for any news.

"What just happened, Katrina all the men raced out of here and said they were going to your aid?" Amy asked.

"We were coming back from the dress fitting and it was getting a little dark. I was talking to Zach in my mind when Abbey screamed. I hit the brakes, luckily, to see a herd of Kangaroos rushing across the road, getting chased by what looked out to be a dragon."

"Did you just say dragon?" Amy asked.

"Yes I did."

"I cannot believe this. I didn't think there were any still here living. I don't mean here as in Australia, but here on the planet," Amy said.

"What does this mean?" asked Miles.

"It means we could have a lot of trouble on our hands. Dragons are known to be reckless and not caring. They were always outsiders and never ones for being around large groups. I just cannot believe it's come out now. Around here of all places, unless it's after the gold we have found in the creeks," Amy said.

"Zach was telling me about that months ago, how the griffin and dragon were similar in that they had a fetish for being around gold. He also told me he liked collecting gold and precious treasures," Kat said, looking around she asked, "where's Alex?"

"He's in the nursery with Jenny, having tea," Sheila said.

Katrina left them and ran into the nursery, to see Alex sitting in a high chair, eating his dinner with Jenny. They all followed her in and looked at her.

"Sorry, that dragon scared me. I had a feeling when it looked at the car that I had seen it before. I am sorry, I think I might just be freaking out a little," Kat said.

"I'll get the brandy!" Miles said, walking back into the lounge. He came back with a cut glass brandy glass, half full for Katrina, and then asked if anyone else wanted one. Katrina drank it down and it seemed to do the trick. She was warming from the inside out and getting pink cheeks.

"I don't think I can take much more of this. It's doing my head in, and to top it off my mother's behaving strange like she is hiding something. Oh, my God! That—"

"Katrina, what is it, dear?" Miles called after her. She found her phone and rang her mother.

"Twin Hills Hotel! Can I help you?" Mary said.

"Hey Mum, is Dad there?"

"Yes, honey, he's in the bar!" her mother said.

"Oh! It's all right, I will talk to him later, Martha's calling."

She put the phone down and relaxed. There were three sets of eyes looking at her.

"I had a horrible feeling that if Mum was hiding something, maybe it was that. That Dad was what we just met on the road."

"Oh! Well, that might explain something, but why would they keep that a secret?" Amy asked.

"I don t know! I hope we can get to the bottom of it."

They suddenly heard cars pulling up and they walked outside to see everyone getting out of their cars, getting dressed, some in underwear and others completely naked. Miles automatically put his hand up in front of Sheila's eyes. Sheila just laughed and smacked his hand back down.

"Always so noble, my love," she said and kissed him on the cheek.

"Did you find anything at all?" Amy called out.

"Yes! But we need to get these children to bed," Richard said.

Katrina took Martha back inside to the nursery and sat her down while she ate her cold spaghetti for tea. Jenny offered to get Alex bathed and took him away. Zach came into the nursery, looking a little worried. He walked over and put a kiss on top of Martha's head and sat down next to Katrina. He put an arm around her waist and squeezed her into him and kissed her on both cheeks and then the lips.

They kissed for a while and then broke apart. When they looked around, Martha was giggling

"What's up with you, Cupcake?" Zach asked.

"Nothing!" she said, giggling.

"Okay. Well, if you have finished your tea, Cupcake, I think it might be your bath time. Come on, let's go." He picked her up and carried her to their bathroom. "Then, after you, it's Mummy's turn," Zach said, laughing.

Once Zach had bathed Martha, read her a short story and put her to bed, he came out of the makeshift bedroom with plans of what he was going to do to Katrina, only to find his father waiting for him.

"Father, everything okay?"

"No, Zach. I am really quite worried. There seems to be a lot of things suddenly happening that we cannot explain. I am just wondering why we suddenly, out of the blue, have a bloody dragon chasing kangaroos in our back yard. We didn't even know they existed. There seem to be a lot more shifters here in this country than I originally thought. I really should have been watching out more for this."

"It's fine, Dad, we will get onto it. I don't think it's suddenly happened. Are you worried that someone saw something with the dingoes?"

"No, it's not that, I just think there's something else happening and I don't know for the life of me what it is. Why would we suddenly have shifters that have not been around for over two hundred or three hundred years? Maybe you could say the same about me? For instance, there were no griffins on the planet, which you are aware of, until I developed!" Zach said. "Mother nature has something in her plans. That's all I can say!"

"Come on, let's go and eat and we can discuss this more with the rest of them and then talk to the others!" Richard said.

They walked off into the dining room to meet up with everyone else. Amy and Sheila were taking the meal out to the table as Miles was opening some bottles of wine.

"I was just saying to Zach that I am a little worried this is the start of something I can't explain. I just cannot comprehend why suddenly a dragon shows up at our bloody door."

"Are you sure that the girls did actually see a dragon?" Amy asked.

Abbey and Katrina looked at each other shaking their heads.

"Oh, I know it was dark, but what I saw through Kat's eyes was a dragon," Zach said.

"Yes, but the weird thing was that when I looked straight at it, it seemed to remind me of something or someone. It's hard to explain," Katrina said.

"Well by the time we got back to where you first saw it, there was nothing but a few heavy footsteps in the paddock, through the mud, leaving a lot of tracks that will be hard to explain, if anyone from the town sees them," Zach said.

"So we have to go along and tidy up for a bloody dragon now?" Aaron asked.

"No, I think it wanted to be seen last night, knowing the girls were coming back from town," Richard said.

"You had better not say the next thing in your head, Zach!" Katrina said, scowling at Zach.

"All I was going to say was that if you guys go anywhere from now on, maybe one of us needs to be with you?"

"I know that's what you were going to say, but come on! Don't you think Abbey and I have been restricted enough coming back here? If you take away even the smallest journeys, you may as well lock us both up."

"That's not a bad idea!" Aaron said, smirking.

"Yeah! Very funny, Aaron. I have a wedding to plan and also, my parents live fifty kilometres down the road. You think they are going to be happy if I stop going in there? My mother's not herself as it is," Katrina said.

"Katrina, I might go and talk to her tomorrow, maybe you and I could go together?" Richard asked.

"Yes, please! There seems to be something going on and I think it's since we told them about the family being shifters. I have asked her again today, at the dressmaker's, but she won't tell me."

"Okay. So, people, we need to spread the word to everyone around, to be vigilant. I don't know whether this dragon is going to show his face again. Knowing the history and manner of these shifters, they don't give a rat's who sees them and we don't need to panic our little town," Richard said.

They finished their meals and then broke away to do their own things, Aaron and Abbey taking off back down to the cabins and Zach and Katrina going back to check on the children.

"I hope Richard can sort my mother out tomorrow! Can he read minds like you?"

"Oh, no. He can do other things, for example he can send out a power around your body, that you can't feel or even see and around a room full of humans. Father can control a whole audience of people or shifters and make them agree with him, or get them to do tasks that they think they are just doing because they want to. He can feel when something is coming good or bad and can read the elements. Why did you ask?" Zach said.

"How is he going to know what's going on in my mother's head if you are not there?" Kat asked.

"Well, you are going to have to wait until tomorrow. In the meantime, I have some spanking to do," Zach said as he grabbed Katrina around the waist and led her to the shower.

"I did promise to give you a bath, as I did Martha, but I have changed my mind."

They walked into the shower and Katrina started to undress, he stood and watched for a while and then slipped out of his clothes. Once they were both naked, he opened the door to the shower for her and turned on the water. As she walked into the cubicle he smacked her on the bottom, she turned and laughed.

"Is that all you have?"

"Oh, I am so glad you asked. That's the beginning." Then he told her what he was going to do with her, inside her head. Just in case the children or anyone else could hear them. Her cheeks went red and she was embarrassed, looking away from him. He laughed and grabbed the soap, covering her back with the cold liquid, then started to massage her back and shoulders. He then moved down to her bottom and gently smacked it again, and grabbed some more soap and moved around to wash her breasts.

She was slowly moaning, enjoying the feel of his hands on her skin. Zach moved down her body until his soapy hand disappeared between her legs; after washing her thighs his fingers found her sensitive clitoris spot and played with it until Katrina was shuddering from the feel he was generating. Her body was so in tune with what he was doing she could climax at any minute. Zach looked straight into her eyes, without his eyes glowing, and told her to stop. She did, but her body was so hard and throbbing. Zach then returned to her breasts squeezing the nipples between his finger tips. He bent down and took one of them in his mouth and happily kissed, sucked and chewed the tip of her nipple until she was so taut and about to burst into a climax, he stopped. He then carried on for another moment in a different spot, until she looked at him and said.

"You're really killing me; I want you so badly."

He stopped teasing her and picked her up. She swung her legs up around his waist and held on to his shoulders. Then he entered her with such a rush all she could do was gasp. He pumped into her again and again until he was pushing her back up against the cold tiles. She held on tight to his waist with her legs, but that position wasn't helping, it was turning her on, until her body started to shake and shuddered climaxing heavily. Her legs had gone to jelly and lost all their strength, but Zach happily held onto her, supporting her body while he moved in and out, pumping and pumping into her like she weighed nothing at all. His eyes appeared to be bronze in colour that meant his griffin was near to the surface and ready to explode out of Zach's body. Only

Zach held his griffin back as he suddenly climaxed hard. His body strained and shaking as he pushed his seed out and into Katrina's waiting warm body. He called out her name and shook violently as he still continued to climax heavily. Breathing quickly, he kissed her on the top of her head. His eyes returned to gold, but his heart was beating so rapidly it was hitting her in the chest.

After a while they managed to come down from their own climaxes and Katrina was put on the floor of the shower to stand again. They rinsed off again before they climbed out of the shower and into the waiting bed, wrapped in towels.

"God! I really needed that!"

"Luckily you could hold me up, I was a mess after the first climax, let alone the second," Katrina said, still breathing heavily.

"You certainly bring out my griffin," he said, laughing.

Chapter 14

The next day Katrina and Richard called in to see her parents at the hotel, they had used the wedding as an excuse. Mary was happy to see them although she was still a little quiet. After a coffee in the bar, Katrina asked her father if they could go through the wine list for the wedding and make sure they had all the correct wine ordered. Charlie and Katrina took off down to the cellar leaving Richard and Mary together.

"Well, how have you been, Mary? Is there anything else you can think about that we need to order for the wedding?" Richard asked.

"No, I don't think so," she said, not reaching his eyes for contact.

"Well if you think of anything at all, please let me know." Richard was sending out his sensors and picking up some real issues that Mary had.

"You really need to talk to me, Mary. I'm here to help you. Come on, you have known me a long time, since we were at college together and I know there's something wrong! What is it?"

"Richard, when we were at college I had a boyfriend. His name was – well, it does not really matter what his name was. Anyway, he seemed to really like me and want to look after me. But suddenly he changed and would get angry at me for no reason. He kept asking me to shift and change into my animal, I told him I didn't know what he was talking about and that he was frightening me. He kept laughing and saying I should

241

know better and being the animal I was supposed to be, wouldn't be frightened of anything."

"So what did he think you were?"

"He would not tell me, kept saying I should know and that it was a part of me. I know it's silly, really quite stupid but that's what he said. I told him that as far as I knew my parents were human and I never knew anything about being a shape shifter or my parents being shape shifters. My parents died when I was really young in a car accident, not far from where we lived. They collided with a road train the driver's last trailer was empty and very light. When he came around the corner he was close to the middle of the road leaving the back third trailer on their side, and the trailer cleaned them up. He didn't even know he had killed my parents until the police stopped him. Some poor tourist following behind my parents saw the whole thing. I ended up living with my mother's parents for over ten years and moving away from that area," Mary said.

"Anyway, the last day I saw him, he walked me from class, insisting that we needed to talk about something and that I should take a walk with him into the woods. That was the same day when you appeared out of nowhere to save me. He couldn't let it go that I didn't know what he was talking about. So he tried to trick me into changing into a shape shifter. He brought the knife out and threatened to kill me if I didn't promise that I would shift, when it got dark. But I couldn't," Mary said.

"Well, he would never have bothered you again because I took care of him. Your boyfriend was a dingo shape shifter and when dingoes try and take on something like a lion they don't normally win.

"When the police came to the college and asked about his disappearance, I can remember one of the class students pointing you out as the girlfriend. The police had turned their entire enquiry on to you. Although I knew you really didn't know what had happened, and that might have been a little bit of my gift to change the way you saw things. When I found out he was a shifter and a dingo, I decided we didn't need anyone else getting hurt in the same way. Dingoes can be evil and intimidating, I haven't met one yet that I have liked," Richard said.

"Only the strange thing was that after that day, I went home back to my grandparents' place and went through my parents' belongings. Which they had kept boxed up down in the cellar. There were journals my father had written and some of them were in a code. When I asked my grandmother if she could read it she declined, telling me to go and ask Poppy. So I asked my grandfather as well and he said it must have been a code that they made up between the pair of them. He didn't really know either, but made a point of telling me that his daughter had fallen head over heels in love with a strange man."

"Well that doesn't sound so bad Mary," Richard said.

"My grandfather went on to tell me that he, my father, had no background that they could follow and everything he had told them did not make any sense. For example, he told them he had grown up in a small town just outside Sydney. But when my grandfather did some checking, the town did not exist, or had not been there for over a hundred years or more. Poppy told me that they were going to run off and elope together if he hadn't given them his blessing. So he told me that they did not want to lose their daughter so they just put up with the lies. As it turned out when he found out my mother was expecting a baby, me he could not have been happier and did everything in his power to protect her. So when I asked my grandfather if he had ever come across shifters, he really didn't understand what I meant. He said I must have been reading too many fairy books or something crazy," Mary said.

"So if your father was a shifter, he hadn't told too many people. Maybe he just told your mother and not them?" Richard suggested.

"So I took the books and kept them safe for years, until I met up with Charlie. When I was carrying the box of books into the house we first rented the bottom of the box fell out. The journals hit the ground and Charlie raced over to help me pick them up. When he saw a book open with its pages flapping and the pictures and some of the coding on them he asked me where I got them. After I explained the whole story he was blown away. He had known about the shifter world since growing up, his best friend was one? Although he could never read it, so I packed the books away and just kept them with me."

"Some humans have been close enough to shifters that they know the secrets of our world."

"Do you still have them?"

"Yes, they are upstairs in the attic. I will go and get them."

"It's all right I will come with you. I can carry them."

They both took off up the stairs to the attic, to find the box hidden under a pile of Christmas decorations. When Richard picked up the box he could feel a slight energy from the books and was excited. Whatever was in these books had a lot of energy, especially if the books had been sitting for over twenty years and not touched.

He carried them to the bar where he opened the box. The first journal he picked up was dated 1230AD, the next 1260AD. He stood back and looked at Mary, his eyes glowing.

"I can't believe you have these they are so old and I can still feel the energy through them. Whoever wrote them was a very powerful shifter. Can you remember who gave them to you?"

"When I moved into the home of my grandparents they told me that they had packed all my parents' belongings from their house in boxes and then stored them away for me. Until when I was old enough to go through them. It was only the books that fascinated me, and there was a little jewellery, which I kept and passed down to Katrina, she used to wear the ring all the time. I'll ask her to show it to you."

"Can I take these books back with me to decipher them? I will keep them very safe."

"Yes, that's fine. Richard, what do you think this means?"

"Well, the only way I see it without reading these books, is that possibly you are from a long line of shifters. When some shifters mate with humans they tend to lose some of their heritage or rather, their pure blood lines. Other shifters need to mate with humans to increase their pure blood lines; it really depends on the breed of the shifter. Sorry, I am not making any sense, am I? The easiest thing to say to you is that you are from shifter heritage, but you can no longer shift."

"Oh, I see now! So, when my boyfriend at school thought I was a shifter, he could not understand why I would not change and show him, because I couldn't physically do it."

"Yes, that sounds about right."

"That explains so much, Richard."

"You would have seen changes in your body by your late teens, early twenties. Charlie should have been able to help you out with that information if his best friend was one," Richard said as Charlie and Katrina walked back in with a few bottles of wine.

"I have got a few samples for us to try tonight, Richard. This is the wine we have decided on. Dad sells a lot so I think it should be all right," Katrina said.

"Okay. Well we had better make a move back to the Ridge, Katrina. When do you need to do the order for the wedding wine, Charlie?" Richard asked.

"Can you let me know over the next few days? I don't want any last-minute hiccups with the delivery. We have a lot of guests coming and we don't want to run out."

"No chance of that, we will order an extra fifty bottles to be sure."

"Oh. Katrina, what did you do with the ring I gave you from my parents?"

"It's back at the Ridge, in my underwear drawer. I took it off when Alex and I came back from our kidnapping. I don't know but for some reason it seemed to be giving me headaches all of a sudden. I thought it couldn't be the ring, but as soon as I took it off my headache eased," Katrina said.

Richard and Mary shared a look, and Richard asked if he could see it when they got home.

They drove back to the homestead and Richard carried the books inside. Katrina, being nosy, picked one up out of the box. "What are these?" she asked but did not get a reply because Richard's eyes were glowing, looking at her as every hair on her head was standing up straight. She dropped the book, looking at Richard.

"What just happened?" she said as they walked into the kitchen.

"I don't know can you do it again?" Richard asked.

Katrina picked up the same book again and held on to it while looking at Richard. Amy, Sheila and Miles all stood opened mouthed in the kitchen, watching as her hair floated freely around in the air.

"Holy crap, what's going on?" Zach said as he walked into the room swinging Martha on his hip. Kat's auburn, long beautiful hair seemed to have collected a lot of static energy and every hair on her head was alive and floating in all directions. It was like Einstein, but not.

Katrina put the book back into the box and watched as her hair settled back down around her shoulders. She walked over to greet Zach and gave him a hug and a kiss, and noticed him jump backwards. Martha's hair was standing on end from the quick kiss and hug she had given Zach. She had not even touched Martha.

"Oh! Shit! Richard, what just happened? I cannot believe this is happening. I need to touch the children and Zach. This is truly mental; can't you make it stop?"

"It's okay, Katrina. Just have a seat over there and sit yourself down and take a few deep breaths, just try and relax. We need to read these books as soon as possible. Can we get Aaron and Abbey up here and anyone else out of the flock that can read old shifter code?" Richard asked.

Three hours later and there was still no joy, each of the eight shifters sitting in the lounge room had not moved from their given spot, spoken or stopped for refreshments.

The journals must have been hard to decipher, as not one of them had finished a journal and started another one. It was making Katrina stressed and irritable, apart from doing her head in. She walked outside for some fresh air, trying to clear her mind. It was not dark yet, although the sun had already disappeared over the horizon. The light from the moon was breaking the surface in the opposite direction towards the cabins.

Without thinking, she followed the pathway down towards the creek. As she was walking along, looking down at the ground, she noticed how the autumn leaves were now drying and changing colours. Some of them were reds and oranges, others were different colours of browns but all just beautiful. Katrina stopped and looked around, and took in the surroundings and then kept walking along. She had a sudden thought of the first night she had seen Zach in the bar, his eyes glowing across the room at her. Then again outside the kitchen at the hotel when he grabbed her and he had told her, she was his, or rather, he said, *'Mine!'* It brought back the nightmare she had had, where she was walking down a path and getting attacked by a huge bird of prey.

She stopped on the path remembering suddenly looking around her heart beating fast, the hair on the back of her neck standing up. She heard a rustling of wings and dared herself to look up; she knew it was a mistake as soon as did. Behind her in the sky she could just see a large dark shadow flying towards her and it looked like it was following. Katrina turned around and thought she would run back towards the house, but it was too late.

Everyone heard her scream from the dining room although by the time they had made it outside she was thirty feet in the air. Instead of the eagle shifter picking her up by the shoulders of her coat, as in her dream, Katrina had been picked up by two large feet with huge claws. As she looked up above her she could see the large body of the dragon. As if knowing she was looking up at him, he gave an echoing roar followed by a small jet of fire out through his mouth. She screamed. They flew for what seemed like ages but would have probably only been ten minutes, until the dragon made a big circle and headed back to the side of a rock face. He then decided to drop her first onto some flat ground, before he circled around again, landing above her on some sharp rocks. He blew a sharp noise out of his giant nostrils and looked down upon her. She thought he sounded like he was almost laughing at her. His eyes were a brilliant green and gold, almost like a lizard's or snake's but his were glowing and hypnotic. His whole body was rippling in blues and greens, almost iridescent and his scales appeared to be glassy with the bright moon, now coming up in the evening sky. She could see a lot more than she did the first night sitting in her car, when he was chasing the kangaroos across the road. He just kept watching her, waiting for what she didn't know. After a while she turned around, swearing at him and found a rock and sat down, this life was getting more bizarre. Luckily she had an open mind; otherwise they would have been visiting her in an institution.

When she looked up again she could see the rest of her family flying around, not close enough to get singed, but close enough to hear what he had to say, if that's what he wanted.

"What the hell do you want? How dare you pick me up like that and frighten the crap out of me. You asshole!" Katrina asked.

She watched as the dragon's body started to shimmer violently, until she was staring at a tall, muscular young man in his late twenties or early thirties. He was gorgeous, with black wavy hair and bright green eyes, only when she looked at him she felt she was looking at her mother. She blinked several times, and still the face was the same. It had to be a relation, there was no other way.

"Who are you? You remind me of my mother but that could not be possible. All her relatives are dead?"

"Not all her relatives. Your mother is Mary Elizabeth Cross, is she not?"

"Maybe! Maybe not!"

"She is married to Charlie Cross and you are Katrina, her daughter. Now engaged to Zach Williams, from the royal shifter family?"

"I suppose I could be!" she screamed at him.

"Don't mess with him, Kat you don't know who he is yet!" Zach said.

"Yes, right, Zach! You come over and sit where I am."

"That's so cute! You actually have little arguments in your head with him," said the stranger.

Katrina was so over all the shit, and walked over to him and asked again: "What the hell do you want? I am getting tired of fucking shifters everywhere. Why am I here, if you are part of my family where the hell have you been until now? If you don't tell me I am going to climb down this stupid fucking rock," Katrina said.

"Wow, that beautiful red hair of yours really does come with a temper and strong attitude," he said, laughing.

Katrina could hear Zach start to growl at the insult the dragon was giving her. He was starting to fly nearer. She stood up and yelled, "Stop there! I can fight my own battles!"

"You belong to me, you and your mother actually!" There was more growling, but she ignored it.

I have been searching for years to find my family. I didn't know where your mother was, until a few weeks ago. After the car accident in which her parents, and my brother died. Mary disappeared, or rather was taken away by her other grandparents when she was only young and I lost track of where she went. They moved several times with his so-called work, not making it easy for me. It was getting harder keeping up with where your mother was. I found out from sources later that Mary had married a human called Charlie, but there was no forwarding address. Then I happened to watch the news one evening a few weeks ago and saw you and the baby on there. I could not believe it when I saw you, the television channel was covering your and the baby's kidnapping. You see you were wearing my brother's ring on your finger, and that's how I recognised you. I tried to send you a message through the ring but it mustn't have worked."

"I took it off, it was giving me headaches. I only said that today to my mother. I have been wearing that ring for years and suddenly it was giving me bad headaches. Weird I thought, but then I looked at my life, and nothing seems to make sense anymore," Katrina said.

"That was me. I was sending you a message through the ring. The champagne diamond and ruby stones combine together acts as a communication stone. I will have to teach you how to use it."

"Well, there's something different, I would never have known that in a million years. So why didn't you just turn up on the front door like a normal person would?" Katrina said.

"Well for a start I am not normal; I am a dragon shifter which means I like to make a scene. I was just hoping to catch you before you got in the car the other night. I really hadn't planned on coming out like that on to the road and scaring you both."

"Well you did! You are lucky I didn't drive the car off the bloody road. That would have been a hard one to tell the insurance company. "Yep! I happened to brake for a freaking dragon chasing a family of kangaroos, across the road. I can just see the men in white coats coming for me, now!" Katrina spat out.

"Wow, my great niece has sarcasm. Who would have thought it? It must be in the blood line."

Another loud growl came from Zach's chest.

"Anyway, like I said before, what do you what? Do you have a name?" Katrina asked, getting irritable.

"Yes I do. My name Christopher Greenwood, but a lot of my friends and associates call me Woody."

There was a lot of noise between her family and the group still flying around some distance away from them. Obviously they recognised his name, but he didn't seem to pick up on that.

"Well, like I said, I want to get to know you and my niece, who I was very fond of all those years ago. I don't think she knows her background and I am sure she is troubled over missing details. In which I would be happy to fill in all the gaps for her."

"If you are my great uncle, how is it that my mother is not a dragon shifter like yourself?"

"I think it's because she was never able to change. Her grandparents were very strict from what I learnt and if she discussed anything strange happening to herself. They just told her to stop reading silly imaginary books, because that's all it was. There must have been something through her teenage years that frightened her enough to close up and not change."

"What you mean is that my mother could have been a dragon shifter as well?"

"Yes, that's what I'm saying!" Woody said.

"Is that why I have different blood than my parents?"

"Did your mother have transplants when she was carrying you?"

"Yes, she said I was making her and myself sick. It's not a common thing but it does sometimes happen, she told me."

"Yes that sounds about right. Not that I have had any children myself."

"Okay. Well I will ring mum when you take me back and you can go visit her. I just have one question?"

"Wow, you only have one! I tell you that you come from a long line of dragon shifters and you only have one question?"

"Well, yes, at the moment! How old are you, because you only look a little older than me?"

"Well, I am not that old, I think I was five hundred and seventy-six on my last birthday, or was it five hundred and sixty-seven? One of those, but I am still young, some dragon shifters have been known to live up to a thousand years."

"You are kidding me? Hey! You might know something about those books that we picked up from my mother's place today and brought back. When I touched one it made my hair full of static," Kat said.

Woody looked at her like she had just delivered some pizza.

"Dad says talk him into bringing you back, he wants to talk to him. We really need to quiz him," Zach said to her.

"Can we go back now, and then I can use my phone to ring mum?"

Woody started to shimmer and before Katrina knew it, she had been picked up and flown back to the Ridge. He popped her down on the cool grass before circling around and landing next to her. There were shifters running in all directions, panicked and not sure what to do.

These shifters had missed her scream in the first place, otherwise they would have known what had been happening. The rest were so shocked all they could do was stand and stare at the gigantic creature that had just landed on their back lawn. Katrina looked around and said to herself, "So much for the security around here!"

Richard appeared from the tree line racing across the lawn followed by Zach and the rest of eagles. Richard stood in front of the dragon and roared at him, still as a lion. If the dragon had wanted to be the dominant one he could have taken the lion on quite easily, turning him in to a char grill but he didn't. Instead he surrendered to the lion, bowing his huge head down onto the grass and that's where he stayed.

Chapter 15

"Wake up, sleepy head!"

"Go away, I am not getting out of bed today."

"Cross, you need to get your ass out of bed, it's getting late. Aren't you getting married today?" asked Abbey.

"No! I changed my mind. I want to stay in bed, there's going to be too many people staring at me."

"Kat you will look beautiful, whatever you decide to wear and I haven't seen the dress yet."

"Do you want me to come in there and spank you? I have time?" Zach called from the hall way.

"No! You stay away from this room, Zachary Williams, you will not see the bride until she walks down the aisle. That's if I can get her hairy ass out of bed!" Abbey shouted.

"Abbey! How dare you! I do not have a hairy ass. Do I, Zach?"

"No! She doesn't but if she doesn't get out of bed soon, I will show you Abbey. When I smack it." They all laughed and Katrina pulled herself out of bed.

"Okay, what's first on the menu?"

"Well we have the hairdresser waiting so if my lady wants to get herself in the shower and wash her hair, we can start. I will go and get your breakfast and bring it back in here. No one is to come in, unless it's your Mother or father, everyone else is out of bounds until the wedding!"

"Wow you are so bossy, I never realised that before. How are the children?"

"Good! Zach is looking after Alex and nearer the time will be in charge of getting him dressed. Mary is looking after Martha over in the guest cabin, and will get her dressed later as well. Don't want that pretty dress covered in Vegemite, do we?"

"I wonder if they slept at all last night, or if they were worrying about their hotel!"

"No I heard on the grape vine this morning that Hailey and Woody were cooking breakfast for all the wedding guest's staying at the hotel. Then they were both coming out later. He seems to have organised everything at the hotel since arriving and basically told them to sit back and relax. So they have taken him up on it."

"Wow! I never thought I would see the day those two took time off. That's great! I was supposed to do that for them when I came back from Brisbane. Only the plans changed and I came back with two children instead."

"Okay, go get in shower. I want you smelling like a rose when I get back!"

Abbey went off to the kitchen while Katrina hopped in the shower.

Two hours later, Abbey, Martha and Katrina's hair were all finished. The hairdresser had tied all of the girls' hair up, in soft curls pinned with emerald flowers to match the bridesmaid's dresses. She had left two long pieces on either side of their faces which were curled into ringlets and left to hang.

Katrina's mother had come in and given Abbey and her daughter some champagne to help with the nerves and finished dressing Martha, who was very excited to be getting all dressed up for the wedding.

Mary herself seemed to have really settled down since her uncle had arrived. It had been quite a shock at the time, for all the family and friends not even knowing dragons existed. After a few weeks of spending some time with him and finding out all the history of her family it had really eased her physically and mentally.

Katrina seemed to be happy for the first time in months, no bad people trying to kidnap her or the children. Her life had actually become quite normal and she was learning all there was to become a dragon shifter if that event ever happened. Although she saw no signs of it happening.

The florist tapped on the bedroom door with all their flowers, she had done a beautiful job on the bouquets. Katrina had asked for a native bouquet which included Orange roses, Pincushion Proteas with green Singapore orchids, and Orange Vanda orchids with succulents. The florist passed Mary her corsage band of fresh Julia roses and green Singapore orchids and then left them.

Mary hugged Katrina and thanked her for the flowers. She sat back with Martha and watched as Julie from the flock transformed their faces into masterpieces with makeup. Julie had also given all three of their nails a coat of gold shimmering nail polish, even Martha, who was squealing in delight.

The next tap on the door was Katrina's father, all dressed up in a tuxedo. He had brought little Alex with him, who still needed his waistcoat. He really did look cute in his black pants, little black shoes and white winged collar shirt. Mary dressed him in his waistcoat and then left them, to go outside to let everyone know they were ready.

Abbey and Katrina hugged and kissed each other and knocked back their champagne.

"Let's do this!"

Abbey and Martha first climbed into their emerald green taffeta dresses whilst Mary helped Katrina climb into her beautiful gold wedding gown. There were a lot of gushes and sighs from the room, when she stood up straight so everyone could see her. The gown was the most beautiful dress she had ever seen. The tight embroidered bodice of sequins and pearls in flowery designs looked better than she thought was even possible. The gown draped down in heavy folds of satin nearly to the floor, with extra length added to the back of the skirt to make a long train. Even her Dad had tears in his eyes when he looked at her.

"Don't you dare start me off, Charlie!" Mary said.

The girls put on their gold slingback sandals and walked out of the bedroom after more hugs and kisses, leaving Katrina and Charlie together alone.

"Now are you sure you want to do this, honey?"

"Yes, Dad, I really do!"

Charlie took Katrina by the hand and walked her through the house until they reached the front garden, which over the past few days had been transformed into an outside chapel. There were lines of white chairs all in rows and flowers tied with ribbons at the two end chairs. Making an aisle for them to walk through, at the end of the aisle Zach was stood waiting with Aaron and Craig on a platform similar to a small stage. There was a large arch covered in Julia roses and more Singapore orchids, it was really a beautiful sight. When Katrina looked back at Zach there were tears falling down his cheeks, he was so emotional it was the first time she had seen him upset. She never took her eyes off him and walked to him, without noticing the crowd of people standing up watching them enter. Katrina thought she would have been nervous, but she was ready and when she saw the look on Zach's face, it made her know she had nothing to fear.

The celebrant welcomed them, and all the guests to the lovely wedding. She then asked them to read their vows out to each other, and then they exchanged their wedding rings. Katrina had bought a beautiful ring for Zach, because he loved gold so much she had picked a band of three different golds (white, rose and yellow). In the centre band, which happened to be the yellow gold, his favourite, she asked the jeweller to add a line all the way around of brilliant cut diamonds.

When he looked down at his finger and then back into her eyes, his eyes said so much. There was so much love and affection in them for her, she needed to swallow the lump in her throat or she would go to pieces and cry like a child.

"Thank you, Kat, that's the most wonderful gift you could have ever given me, apart from giving me our own child," Zach had said into her mind.

"Well, we might have to work on that, later!" she said back to him, smiling from ear to ear as he slid her wedding ring on. They only heard what the celebrant was saying by chance.

"I now pronounce you husband and wife, you may kiss your bride," the celebrant said.

They kissed as husband and wife for the first time passionately while a cheer went up all over the Ridge! They were surrounded by guests and family kissed, hugged and welcomed to the different families. None of Charlie's family knew they were surrounded by shifters and Richard wanted to keep it that way. Katrina's uncle came up and hugged her, and whispered something in her ear only with the noise of other guests she couldn't hear him.

She had watched him go and say something to Richard but was not sure what he had said to her to start with. As there were guests and flock members everywhere who were congratulating them she couldn't stop and follow him. Even the florist had stayed to congratulate them both and make sure everything went well.

It was a lovely wedding and it had all been a lot of work, she only had to look around to see the work all the guys had put in to make it perfect for her and Zach. Miles and Sheila came up and hugged them both. Katrina loved these two so much for staying with her and the children. She couldn't thank them enough for everything they had done and for looking after the children for her while they celebrated.

After the family photographs were all taken Zach had the photographers go around taking photos of everyone else at the wedding. He decided now was a good enough time to start that data base.

An hour later the food started to arrive on stainless steel trays carried on the arms of waiters. The trays were full of canapés. Some smoked salmon mascarpone and dill. Others trays displaying different cold meats and cream cheeses, the variety was outstanding. There were also chicken drumsticks in an array of different marinades. There were trays of oysters, raw and cooked, in Mornay or Kilpatrick sauces, fresh prawns and mud crab.

The champagne flowed and there were a lot of speeches, well into the evening. The food kept coming through the evening until the guests started to come up to them and say goodbye. By nine o'clock a lot of the wedding guests had already gone, Hailey had taken Charlie's relatives back to the hotel as most of them would be leaving in the morning. The remainder of the party was mainly the shifters that had stayed and carry on celebrating as the alcohol didn't seem to worry them the same. After Katrina walked back outside from seeing off more of her guests, she noticed that there was a particular female talking to Zach and Craig. It didn't seem to worry her until this guest started running her hand up and down Zach's arm.

"What the hell is that chick doing?" she asked Zach inside her head to him.

"Nothing! Honey. She is just flirting a little bit she's always been like that. She's an old girlfriend. I think she's keen on Craig."

"Well, why the hell is she touching you all over the arm and not Craig?"

"I am not sure. I can tell her to stop?"

"You'd better, before I rip her head off!"

"Katrina, it's nothing really – Katrina?"

All of a sudden, Katrina started to see red, her vision changing. Instead of colours it was like she was looking through red lenses on a pair of reading glasses. She went to walk away from everyone just as her uncle came around the corner. He saw she was suddenly in distress and asked her if she was all right?"

"Why am I getting so angry at the female flirting with my brother and new husband over there? I really want to kill her, and she's not really doing anything except touching my husband!"

"Katrina, you need to take some deep breaths. I said to you earlier that I thought someone was going to make you angry."

"Oh, is that what you said? I couldn't hear because everyone was cheering at us?" Katrina asked.

"Yes! I said that I had a horrible feeling that someone was going to upset the balance tonight, and that's why I went over to Richard and asked him if he felt it too?"

"And Richard said what, exactly?"

"He said he knew there was going to be a shifter here tonight that was going to cause trouble and that he hoped it would be after all the humans left."

"Well, I really feel like shit, I am seeing red in front of my eyes and my whole vision has changed. I seem to be looking down a telescope or something! What does that mean?"

"Oh! Shit! Katrina, I know it's your wedding night and all that, but you really need to come with me! There are still a few humans over there, I think you are about to shift."

"Shift! You're not making any sense, uncle! You really need to help me my head is seriously throbbing."

"Katrina I mean shape shift! Like into a dragon!"